P9-DCD-650

SOMEONE TO LOVE

A NOVEL

by

GAIL KIRACOFE

MASSANUTTEN REGIONAL LIBRARY
Harrisonburg, VA 22801

F.
Kir

This is a work of fiction. All characters and events are fictitious; figments of the author's imagination. Any resemblance to persons living or dead is coincidental.

All rights reserved. This book or any portion thereof may not be reproduced or used in any manner whatsoever without the express written permission of the author.

Copyright 2013 by Gail Kiracofe

ISBN-13: 978-1484960059

ISBN-10: 148496005X

Acknowledgments

Special thanks to the members of my Writers Group who helped me through the process of creation. And blessings on the early draft readers for their encouragement and valuable suggestions. Without them this book would still be tucked away in a drawer. Also, hugs for niece Julie Gilbert whose name I 'borrowed' for one of my characters and for niece Heather Kersh who thought I should send the manuscript straight to Oprah. Now *that's* love!

There is only one happiness in life, to love and be loved.

~George Sand~

Chapter 1

One snappy February day I drove home down Ivy Road feeling happy and relaxed, like a turtle on a log in the sun. I was tired after my weekly T'ai Chi class and thinking a cup of hot tea sounded good. The Rav-4 skidded a bit on the thin layer of snow as I turned into my driveway. I waved at Howard, my next-door neighbor, as he swept the snow off his sidewalk, his head engulfed in a breathy cloud. I called a cheery 'hello' across the street to Jenna who was looking in her mailbox. In mine I found just fliers and other trash which all got dumped into the first waste basket I passed on my way to the kitchen. But then a letter, tucked in the middle, caught my eye. I stooped to pick it out and saw the return address. Federal Corrections Facility. My nice 'turtle on the log' feeling gave way to the sense that a tidal wave was about to sweep that poor turtle off the log into murky, churning waters.

I made some tea and settled at the table. Molars clenched, stomach churning, I contemplated the letter. This was one of many I'd received during my son's eight years in prison. My physical response was always the same, making for ground down teeth, and chronic diarrhea. But the time for his release was coming soon and with no other place to go, he'd have to come here. I looked at the letter some more. Finally I propped it against the sugar bowl and left it there, unopened. The cup of tea remained untouched as well.

As I often do when I am troubled, I went for a brisk walk. My street, Ivy Road, was a quiet oasis between busy boulevards. I loved it there. Swimming pools, gym sets, dog runs, and workshops are tucked into large backyards hidden behind the '50's built, mostly red brick homes. My three bedroom rancher sat in the middle of the block between Howard Thompson's two story colonial on one side and the Newberrys' meticulously kept Cape Cod on the other. Jenna and Jim Barr lived across the street in a cute Craftsman style home. Azalea bushes set their yard ablaze with pink blooms in the spring and I always enjoyed that view. My neighbors were friendly, but busy with their own lives, and didn't fraternize much. Well, except for Howard. He mowed old Mrs. Markowitz's lawn in the summer and shoveled her sidewalks and driveway in the winter. He repaired Bobby Ortiz's bike on a regular basis, and consulted with Mr. Newberry about the best dates for starting their spring vegetable gardens. He'd even taught me about molly screws when he replaced a towel bar in my bathroom one time.

"Beep, beep, Mz. Fischer, here I come." I jumped aside just as Bobby wobbled past me on his bike. At only four years old he was still a bit unsteady.

"You're doing great, Bobby. Keep it up." I remembered when Jack was that age and just learning, too. How dear he had been to us, scraped knees and all. He'd been bright, cute, funny, loving. Where had that gone? I sighed and accelerated my pace.

By the time I'd walked the length of Ivy Road a couple of times and done a bit of deep breathing, my jaw relaxed and my stomach returned to normal. I resolved to be as kind to Jack when he got home as I could be, to not let him push my anger buttons, and to work together to make his transition as easy as possible.

That night I had a troubling dream. A black dog, tethered by a chain, snapped and snarled in my backyard. Its barking awakened me, but stopped when I got up to go to the bathroom. Before returning to bed I pulled back the curtain and looked out. The backyard lay serene in the moonlight, its blanket of pristine snow unbroken except for tiny footprints under the bird feeder. There was no black dog there.

***

The next day low clouds foretold more snow and the temperature hovered just below freezing. I got up early, showered, and dressed in black woolen slacks and a white turtle neck under a navy blue blazer. I made my bed and cooked some hot cereal for breakfast. The letter on the table nagged at my conscience while I ate, but I couldn't bring myself to open it.

About nine o'clock, hoping to miss rush hour traffic, I donned my warmest coat and left the house for the interstate to drive to my volunteer job at the Teen Moms Center. It's located toward downtown Midsouth City in an area I think of as a battle zone, with dilapidated rooming houses, deserted stores, and trash strewn parking lots. Gradually, after about a mile, that dreary area gives over to tall buildings of commerce and government, good hotels, gothic churches and ornate theaters; the ingredients of a thriving city. But in the battle zone low income government housing projects bunch along the elevated highway like barnacles on the sides of a decaying boat. Here drugs are rampant, violence an everyday event, and hope pretty much nonexistent. The interstate carries thousands of commuters, blind to the chaos below, into the city in the morning and home to the serenity of the suburbs in the evening.

I slipped my Toyota between a Caddy and a Saab, and turned off the interstate at an exit in the midst of the projects. The ramp put me on Lincoln Street where I turned left and drove six blocks, between the Roosevelt Project and Cummins Homes. Beyond them was a shabby neighborhood of small shops, store front missions and rubbish littered sidewalks. Past the Union Mission, Smokey's Ribs Café, the Clean Duds Laundromat, and a Salvation Army store, I found a slot, pulled into the curb and parked. I pulled the hood of my parka over my head, and mindful of the icy sidewalk, carefully stepped through my visible breath to the doorway of a grungy looking storefront. A small hand printed card taped at eye level on the glass door said 'Teen Moms Center'. I entered a large room with a couple of desks in an area near the door and walled off cubicles filling most of the rest of the room. I said good morning to Martha, the receptionist, and put my coat on our shared old fashioned hall tree in the corner. After I tucked my purse in a drawer in my desk I walked down the hallway to say hello to my friend, Myra Boutwell, one of the social workers. We chatted for a minute then I returned to my desk, turned on my computer, and started to work.

For almost a month I'd been doing data entry work for this agency that serves unmarried, pregnant teenagers, most of them from the government housing projects nearby. After directing a non-profit organization myself that depended on volunteers to get the job done, I knew the value of this relatively mindless, but none-the-less important task I performed for Teen Moms. And let's face it, the lack of pressure was refreshing.

The morning was well along when the door banged open letting in a blast of wintry air. I continued to tap away at my keyboard until the sharp smell of ozone touched my nose. I looked up.

"May I help you?" I asked of the very pregnant young girl edging around the desk. Our clients usually check in with the receptionist and then go on to one of the cubbies to visit their social worker.

A dark hand reached toward the desk drawer. "You got enythin' to eat in there?"

"No!" I said, pushing the rough, icy hand away. "Why? Are you hungry? When did you eat breakfast?"

"Breakfast? I don't call no cold sweet 'tater breakfast."

"You only had a cold sweet potato for breakfast?" This waif, this very pregnant urchin, stood there wearing a faded cotton dress, a thin sweater that did not begin to stretch across her belly and worn canvas shoes with no laces and no socks. Her dusky eyes were watering, from sadness or from the cold, I couldn't tell.

"I only had a piece of it. My two little brothers ate the rest." Those eyes ripped the heart right out of my plump old breast.

"Oh, my goodness." I reached into another drawer and pulled out my purse. "There's a café across the street. Take this, and go get yourself something good to eat." I thrust some bills into the girl's hand.

"My sister out there is hungry, too, maybe you could...?"

I peered through the store front window and saw another child shivering in the blustery day. I reached into my purse again and added another bill to my already generous donation. Instantly, the woeful waif turned into an exuberant imp, dancing out the door, laughing and calling back, "Thanks old lady! Thanks!"

I watched as the two girls pulled on warm coats and scarves from a pile hidden below window level, removed their canvas shoes, and plunged their feet into scruffy boots. Waving gaily they marched away, triumphantly swinging the bag carrying their disguises between them.

Martha snickered.

I'd been had! Roberta Fischer, intelligent, retired but not "old", former director of her own non-profit agency had been conned. No other word for it. Conned. I sat back in my chair and laughed.

* * *

Myra and I walked to Smokey's Café at noon. I never knew whether the name Smokey's applied to the owner's name or to the dusky aroma that swallowed you at the door. The place was packed tight at lunch time so we stood in line and shouted above the hubbub. I told her about the girl who'd conned me.

"Oh, dear. That's Kenisha Johnson, our pint-sized panhandler." Myra grinned at me, her dark eyes alive behind stylish rimmed glasses. "I forgot to warn you. She pulls that 'cold sweet potato' ploy on all our new volunteers. I'm sorry. I hope you didn't invest too much."

Finally settled at a table, we gave our orders. Myra looked nattily professional in a tailored black pantsuit with a bright red blouse, the antithesis of 'social worker'. We'd met at a seminar where her stories about 'her girls' had intrigued me. A few months earlier when I was feeling the need for a new challenge in my life I called her and offered my services.

I continued our conversation. "I don't mind the money but she called me 'old lady'! That, I cannot have."

Myra responded with a wry chuckle and one raised eyebrow.

"Tell me about her." I flipped open my napkin and picked up my spoon as the waitress delivered our food.

Myra opened her sandwich to inspect and delicately rearrange the interior. "It's the same old story. Kenisha lives in the projects with her mother, an addict, who is a single mom with a bunch of children by different fathers. The men hang around all day and pretty soon the children are having children. It's an endless cycle." She sighed and took a bite of her sandwich and a sip of hot tea. "Kenisha has a high IQ and we are trying to see that she gets a taste of life beyond the projects. Some of the other girls, too, of course."

My hot vegetable soup smelled good and tasted better. I crushed some saltines into the bowl to cool it down a bit. Smokey's didn't lend itself to perfect table manners. "I don't understand why they do it. Why have babies when there is no father, no money, and no way to get out of there?"

"The girls will tell you," Myra replied, "because that's the only way to have something to love that will love you back."

The next day I went on with my usual routine, still ignoring the letter sitting like a spider on the kitchen table. At the monthly 'Koffee Klatch' of the Newcomers Club old members and new arrivals nibbled on goodies and sipped coffee. The hostess proudly showed off her home, one of those huge new houses with no yard, but boasting an indoor swimming pool and a special fitness room with weights and a treadmill and stationary bikes. Like New York City, it was a nice place to visit but I wouldn't want to live there. We gathered in the 'parlor', settled on expensive-looking sofas and chairs and introduced ourselves. Each person told where they'd come from and how many children and grandchildren they had. One woman even mentioned her son the doctor, another, her daughter the astronaut. Well, not really, but you get the picture.

When it was my turn I said, "I'm Roberta Fischer. Single, well, divorced, actually. I moved here about ten years ago. I recently started to volunteer at the Teen Moms Center, and I'm on the board of SNIP, an animal rescue and spay/neuter organization. Oh! And I also play the recorder with a group that performs for nursing homes and churches and places like that. I don't have any children, or naturally, any grandchildren."

I always hated to lie, but what could I say? "My son is in a Federal prison in Illinois. He tried to rob a bank, which is a federal offence, you know. Before, he was just in local jails and state prisons. He's working his way up, you see." Yeah, right.

Carrying my coffee cup I mingled. "You're certainly a busy lady," an old gal wearing a purple hat commented.

"Oh well, it keeps me off the streets and out of the bars, as my ex used to say." She faked a small laugh, raised an eyebrow, and moved on. Some people have no sense of humor. I drifted from group to group, searching for an interesting conversation to join. My age group was telling adorable grandchildren stories, while the soccer moms talked school plays and music recitals. The married folk were discussing stuff I didn't want to hear about, so I left early and went home to eye that stupid letter some more. I still didn't open it.

On Saturday I avoided looking at the letter sitting like a poisonous toad on the kitchen table as I left the house to meet my friend Julie for coffee at the local latte place.

I found a parking place on the street and walked to CuppaJava, tucked between a barber shop and a vintage clothing store. The usual Saturday jeans-clad crowd was gathering to get their morning caffeine fix. The rich smell of brewing coffee and hot muffins created a 'momma's kitchen' atmosphere. Julie was waiting for me at a small table near the window, a mocha latte topped with whipped cream grasped between her hands. "How goes it?" she said.

"Let me get something and I'll be right back." Julie Gilbert was my best friend, someone I'd met a few years before when I volunteered to do some publicity for her animal rescue group. We hit it off immediately and later learned we each have an adult child with addiction problems. Julie grew up in a hippy commune and was probably the smartest person I've ever known. My middle-class Hoosier background seemed humdrum in comparison.

"OK, now. With some cappuccino and biscotti, I may be able to face the day." I draped my coat across the back of a chair, sat down and looked at my friend. Well-worn blue jeans on Julie's slender body were a fashion statement that my own baggy pants could never claim. Always thrifty, her faded maroon sweat shirt that said 'Harvard' was probably picked off a table at a rummage sale. Feet clad in red high top tennis shoes were propped on an adjoining chair. A wild bush of curly red hair surrounded her narrow face. Green eyes bored into mine, an unnerving habit of hers.

"I got another letter from Jack,"

"Oh? What'd he say?" She had some whipped cream on her upper lip and licked it away.

"I don't know. I haven't opened it."

"Why's that?"

I sighed. "Because it'll be filled with lists of things he wants me to do. Or with updates on the lawsuit he's trying to file against the prison system. Or with his very unrealistic plans for when he gets out." I crunched on my biscotti.

"I see what you mean." She bit into her blueberry muffin, but kept her eyes on me, waiting for me to go on.

"And he always blames all of his misfortune on me or anyone else he can think of. Listen, Julie. I'm past the place where I want to be upset by my kid. He's almost 50. Not a kid anymore. Trouble is I feel awful that I'm not looking forward to having him here. I'm a terrible person, I guess."

"Oh, yeah, really evil. That's you." Julie shook her head. Sitting back in her chair she added, "You're a dumb shit, do you know that?"

"I hardly ever talk about this stuff with anyone else so it's nice to have someone who understands. Even if she cusses and says ver' cruel things sometimes." We laughed, a bit ruefully, I thought.

"Yes, well, unfortunately, I've 'been there, done that' with Kimmy," said Julie. "I've seen her drunk and high and I've bailed her out more times than I can remember. It's tough."

"You have to wonder if they can ever change. Jack's getting older now and I just get so mad when I think that he's wasting a perfectly good life. He's not dumb. Just stupid, I guess."

"Did you ever think he might have a mental disorder of some kind?" asked Julie.

"No, he's really smart, like I said. But he's an alcoholic and a drugaholic, I suppose, if that's what you call it."

"Intelligence does not necessarily rule out mental disorders, Roberta. You might want to see what you can learn about them."

I ignored her but filed that information away for future cogitating. Not right then, though. I changed the subject.

"Let me tell you about this kid named Kenisha I met at the Teen Moms Center. Can you believe she conned me out of ten bucks? She's six months pregnant, only 14 years old, and is going to drop out of school when the baby comes. But if she's clever enough to con me, you'd think she'd be clever enough to want more from her life."

I went on to describe Kenisha, and how she and her friend had worked the con. "I just feel there is something there, something in her that can maybe get her out of that housing project. Is that dumb?"

"No," Julie replied. "It isn't dumb, but it may be difficult. What are you thinking?"

"Oh, I don't know. If she'd give up the baby she wouldn't have to quit school, but there's a snowball's chance in hell she'll do that. Maybe I can help her see things differently, though. I'm going to try, anyway."

We finished our coffee, gave each other a hug, and parted ways.

Tail down, crouching, quivering, eyes boring into mine, the black mastiff braced, ready to lunge. He bared long, sharp teeth and a growl rolled from deep within its throat, but the wall at my back refused to budge. I turned sideways and covered my face with my hands. Arms and elbows protected my throat and chest. I started my last prayer… "Oh, God…."

I woke in a sweat and lay shivering in a tangle of bedding. That dream again. That damn dream, again.

After a shower and hair wash I sat at the kitchen table with a glass of juice, a cup of coffee, and a hardboiled egg. The letter remained unopened, propped against the napkin holder. How many more days could I ignore it? One more at least, I decided. Stamped with the Federal

Correction Facility return address, I knew who it was from, and could almost surely recite exactly what it said:

Dear Mom,

I'm going to need some more money. You would not believe what they charge for the things I need like cigarettes, shampoo, sodas, and snacks. I will be so happy to get out of here and come home to be with you. It should be pretty soon, now. I will let you know. Love, Jack

I'd received dozens of such letters over the past seven or so years. At first they emphasized his innocence, the horrors of prison life, at least those that would get past the prison censors. And then a litany of his plans for the future, all terribly unrealistic, and needing several thousand dollars of start-up financing. From me, of course. The very thought of his homecoming drained me.

On Monday at the Teen Moms Center I kept a watch out for Kenisha. Finally she appeared, slipping through the door, avoiding my eyes and my desk. Her pregnant body was layered with mismatched sweaters and a thread-bare coat, her head wrapped in a ratty-looking scarf. Booted feet scraped along the floor. Her stance was proud, however, as she approached Martha's desk.

"Young lady!" After years as an agency exec my voice was commanding.

"Yes-um?" Her eyes looked everywhere but at me.

"Come sit down here, and talk to me, please." I reached into a drawer and slid a small paper bag across the desk. "That's a muffin, in case you're hungry again."

Her laugh fluted skyward. "You OK, lady. Thanks." She scuffed across from Martha's desk and slipped into the chair beside mine. She peeked into the bag, then closed it. "I'll take it home to share with my little brothers."

Leaning forward I looked at the pregnant child. "It's Kenisha, isn't it?"

"Yes'um." For the first time those intelligent dark eyes peered directly into mine.

"My name is Mrs. Fischer. How old are you, Kenisha?"

"I'm 15," then seeing the look on my face she amended, "...uh, 14, but I'm almost 15."

"When's your baby due?"

"In May. Three more months." Kenisha replied.

"Hmmm. That must be a little bit scary."

"Yes-um, but I'm real excited about having a baby."

Wanting to hear it for myself, I probed. "And why is that?"

Kenisha looked at me as if I'd suddenly grown a second nose. "Why, everyone wants a baby!" She repeated Myra's words almost exactly, "It's the only way to have something to love that will love you back!"

For a moment I pondered her declaration. "But what about school?"

Kenisha shrugged her thin shoulders. "Can't go to school, no more, after the baby comes."

"Wouldn't you like to?"

Kenisha gave that some thought. "Why? Don't need to know 'bout history and math and stuff to be a momma." She paused. "But I'll miss it, I s'pose."

Ah! Did I detect a chink in the armor? "Ms. Boutwell has asked me to go along on the trip to the museum on Saturday. Are you going?"

"That's dumb. Don't wanna go to no museum. Just see old stuff." Kenisha snorted her disdain.

"Have you ever been to a museum?"

"No, ma'am."

"Oh, come on. It will be fun, and I happen to know we're going to get lunch afterward."

That got her. "Well…mebbe," she mumbled.

"Good! I'll see you then."

"I gotta go see Mz. Boutwell now. Bye…Mz. Fischer."

I watched as she shuffled down the hallway, a little girl who knew too much, and yet so little.

Chapter 2

Ivy Road twinkled with evening lights reflecting on fallen snow as I neared home. It was a lovely, peaceful scene, almost like a greeting card. Just one house in the block clung to a remnant of Christmas spirit; tiny multi-colored lights twinkled bravely from a spindly spruce tree near the front door. If the owners didn't disrobe the tree by St. Patrick's Day they could be the recipients of the neighborhood association's 'Irma Bombeck Award'. I smiled, remembering the year I won when my 4th of July display of red, white, and blue streamers, flags, and a cardboard Uncle Sam wilted in the summer weather to sodden lumps on the lawn by Labor Day. After that I kept my outdoor decorating to one classic wreath on the front door at Christmas time. Simple is better as one ages I was learning.

My house was dark and the outside security light failed to come on when I drove into the carport. "Damn! I forgot to replace that bulb…again." Keys in hand, I toed my way around the corner of the house toward the back door. No twinkling lights here. I edged forward, poking my foot ahead of me to find the steps. Instead my boot hit something soft. Something soft, and large. Something soft and large… and moving.

"That you, Mom?" it said. "Where ya been?"

When I touched earth again after a short flight straight up, I screeched, "Jack! Omigosh! You scared me to death! What are you doing here?"

"I'm not sure. Sleeping it off, I guess." The words slurred from his mouth. "Dincha' get my letter?"

I stepped over him, unlocked the door and pushed my way into the kitchen. I flipped on the lights, and turned to look at him, still sprawled at the bottom of the steps, his back to me.

A very short, very bad haircut revealed a three inch scar resembling a fuzzy red caterpillar on the back of his skull. He wore thin khaki pants, topped by a lightweight tan jacket over a thin white t-shirt, his only defense against the bitter evening. Stiff new leather shoes covered his feet but his boney ankles were left bare to fend for themselves. A canvas gym bag on the ground beside him seemed to be his only luggage.

I ignored his question, but I couldn't ignore the guilt that engulfed me. "It's warm in the house, honey. Can you get up and come in?" A stray cat could not have looked more pitiful.

I went back down the steps, took his elbow and helped him into the kitchen. "Sit here at the table and I'll make us some tea." But first I grabbed my mother's old woolen afghan from the back of my recliner in the den and wrapped it around him along with a hug. "There, that should warm you up." A couple of day's growth of beard shaded his cheeks and felt prickly on mine. His breath stank of cigarettes and whiskey.

"Thanks, Mom." He pulled the afghan over his ears and grinned his old boyish grin, looking like a sappy turtle. New parenthesis-like grooves bracketed his mouth, and a gap in his teeth shocked me. The last time I saw that void he was just seven years old. My handsome son had aged but not gracefully. Quite painfully, apparently. I walked past the table to start the tea. The unopened letter on the table loomed large. I snapped it up and jammed it in my pocket, hoping he didn't see. I made a big fuss of filling the kettle and getting mugs from the cupboard.

"I'm so sorry I wasn't here. Did you have to wait long?"

"I stopped at 'The Pumps'. Maybe I had one too many. Makin' up for lost time, y'know." He giggled and looked around the kitchen as if to reassure himself that this was indeed the home he remembered.

I followed his gaze and saw the faded red-plaid curtains at the window, the same as when he went away. I'd never kept a neat kitchen so my counters were loaded down with small appliances, an open cookie jar, even some dirty dishes. A pan of cold soup sat on the stove. Admittedly the place smelled, at best, stale.

I smiled at him. "Same old place. Are you hungry?" I poured the tea and pushed the sugar bowl to him. "I could warm up that soup. It's homemade vegetable. Or how about a cookie?" I moved the almost empty container to the table.

"Naw. I just want to get warm then hit the sack. I was on that crappy bus for 12 hours. Stop and go. Stop and go. It was a bitch." His voice elevated, the pitch rising with his temper and the flush of red on his face.

His familiar freckled hands gripped the mug. Wrinkled and scarred now, they bore a tattooed letter at the base of each finger. When he saw me looking, Jack quickly tucked his hands into the pockets of his jacket. For the first time our eyes met and held.

Neither of us spoke. I tried to see inside his head to understand the changes so obvious on the outside. But his eyes were opaque, giving off no light, and barring me from entering his hidden chamber of prison horrors. I could only imagine what he was seeing in return.

A judgmental old witch, I supposed, and not the heartsick, guilt-ridden mother I really was. The silent exchange cemented the barrier between us that would take me months to breach.

The happy homecoming scene changed quickly, re-minding me of his violent mood swings before he went to prison.

"You shunta left me out in the cold like that, Mother. You didn't even read my letter, did you? I saw it there." He looked close to tears, but ducked his head so I could-n't see.

"I'm sorry, honey. It's just that I….."

"I'm going to bed," he said abruptly.

"Jack…" Before I could continue he pushed back from the table, tipping over the chair and leaving the mug of tea untouched. He snatched a cookie out of the jar and, still bundled in the afghan, lumbered down the hallway to the room that was his before he went to prison.

"Well, OK, then," I called after him. "If you need anything just let me know." The bedroom door closed firmly. He couldn't hear my "Good night then, and I'm glad you're home." Even to me it sounded weak. I wiped away the tear that was tickling its way down my cheek and pulled his letter from my pocket. Scribbles on a small piece of paper said:

Mom,

I'm being released next week, and I think I will be able to get home on the bus by Friday. I'll call you when I get in, or if I have enough money, I'll take a cab home.

I love you, Jack

I sipped my tea and waited for it to warm my heart. When that didn't work I began to clean the kitchen. I started by righting the over-turned chair. I had known this was coming. Jack was in prison for nearly eight years for trying to rob a bank. He copped a plea, as they say, and got eight years instead of the twenty-five he might have received if he were found guilty at trial. The story was almost humorous, or would have been if it hadn't starred my own son.

He and a buddy selected a small bank just across the street from a large grocery chain. While Jack entered and held up the bank his buddy was supposed to stay in the car ready to zoom off when Jack emerged with the loot. The buddy got cold feet and fled the scene, leaving Jack literally holding the bag. In desperation he ran across the street and into the grocery store where he huddled in the men's room until the police came and arrested him. His picture appeared on the front page of the newspaper the next morning, and again that evening on the TV news. He was grinning as they hauled him off to jail. A mother's proudest moment.

I dumped the soup down the disposal, ate the last Oreo and put the cookie jar away.

My emotions were a tangled mass, like the electrical cords behind my computer desk. The ones I struggled to hide as best I could. I loaded the dishwasher and washed by hand the plastic and wooden things it wouldn't take. Put them away. Tossed out an empty cereal box.

It made me mad that I had to go through all this one more time. That's an admission of selfishness I tried to hide, even from myself. But I'd endured his childhood with its unending behavior crises, his troubled young manhood spent in an alcohol and drug induced haze, and now to face yet another struggle to help him reinvent himself in an alien world....when would it all end? Or perhaps the question was 'would it all end?'

I wiped off the small appliances and stowed them away in the lower cabinet where they belonged. Swiped at some dirty fingerprints on the cabinet door.

I felt sad because my son was wasting his life away. He was in his forty's now, a time when other mothers were reporting on their children's rise in their professions, or advancements at work, or on finding the love of their lives, or at the very least that they were hitting the golf ball better. No wonder I lied and told strangers I had no children. No wonder I slipped away from conversations like that to go to the ladies room, or out the door to go home. The pain was less that way. I desperately wanted Jack to be happy but so far that was a wish unfulfilled.

I scrubbed down the counters and stove. Wiped off the canister set and threw out the dead ivy sitting on the window sill.

My frustration felt like practicing a scale on my recorder over and over and over again, never to get it right. In spite of all my efforts to help Jack by offering advice, or advancing money, or providing basic necessities like a home and clothing and meals, nothing ever changed. This didn't go on for a few weeks or months – it was going on for a lifetime. If I couldn't perfect playing the scale on my recorder I'd have thrown it out the window. Sometimes I felt like doing the same to Jack.

I swept and mopped the floor. Leaned out the back door and shook the braided rug, spreading blots of dirt on the blanket of snow.

I'd been cheated out of the joys of parent-hood. And that felt like betrayal to me. I wasn't fool enough to believe that my life should be perfect or even close to it. But we adopted a child in order to enjoy him. Now, when my friends were dandling darling grandchildren on their knee, or happily planning zoo days, or family gatherings, I sat home alone. I could only wonder where in hell my kid was and what kind of trouble he'd found now, or even more likely, how much money he'd ask for the next time he called.

Add it all together and what I got, unfortunately, was anger. Sometimes smoldering, sometimes flashing hot, but always simmering, just below the surface.

A last sweep of air freshener and I was done. Surveying my work I was pleased with the result. It certainly smelled better, and I just wished that helping to clean up Jack's life could be as easy. I knew it was up to me to find ways to make life better for him. I just didn't know what those ways were. I hadn't been to my support group at Al-Anon for quite a while but I remembered some things they taught.

"Set boundaries, you must set boundaries," they would say. I was sure of it.

Reaching into a nearby drawer I pulled out a pen and some paper and made a list.

1.) No drinking. 2.) No drugs 3.) At home by 11 p. m. 4.) Get a job!

With a sigh, I turned off the lights and went to bed. My last thought before I fell asleep was that now Jack's imprisonment was over and mine…mine was just beginning…again.

In the morning a noise in the hall bathroom brought me up out of the sheets.

I slipped on a robe, stuffed my toes into scuffs and stepped into the hall. The bathroom door was open. Jack stood over the toilet, still dressed in the rumpled clothes of the night before. Dry heaves shook his body. "Sorry," he said. Dark whiskers covered his pale cheeks and he smelled awful.

"Oh, dear. That's not good. I'll be right back," I said. "I'll get you something to make you feel better."

I remembered too well the antidote to a night of drinking. In the kitchen I put on the large coffee pot, and began concocting the 'a little of this and a little of that' cocktail his dad developed over the years for his own 'little problemo'.

When I got back Jack was sitting on the floor, his legs encircling the toilet. I handed him a plastic cup and he sipped cautiously from the 'Fischer's Fix' I knew he had seen Steve drink countless times.

"Alright now, get out of those clothes and into the shower. Put your clothes in the hall here and I'll put them in the washer for you. I think you'll find some of your old clothes in your room. There's coffee in the kitchen when you're ready."

"Yeah, OK." He took hold of the sink and pulled himself up and I returned to the kitchen.

I could hear the shower running and it brought back memories. When Jack was a boy he revealed to me one day that if I told him to take a shower he'd stand under the spray while he counted up to fifty. If I told him to take a 'really good' shower, he'd stand there till he count-ed to one hundred. "No soap?" I'd asked.

"Nope." His smile was of the 'cat that ate the canary' variety.

The coffee had perked and the washer was half way through its cycle when Jack came down the hall.

"Like my tattoos?"

I was pouring him a cup of coffee and said, "I put your clothes in the washer."

"I said 'do you like my tattoos?'"

I turned around to look. Jack's hair was wet from the shower and his jeans were riding low on his hips as he stood there barefooted, carrying a shirt in his hand. What I saw shocked me. His chest, neck, and arms to the wrists were covered with an astonishing array of prison art.

Without thinking I blurted, "Oh, Jack. That's, that's… hideous. You'll have to wear long sleeves to apply for a job." I felt like crying. He'd been such a beautiful little boy.

Jack looked as if I'd slapped him. "Leave it to you, Mom. I just got out of that fucking prison and you want me to go get a job today. I'll get a job when I'm good and ready. And for your information tattoos are very big these days, and not just in prison."

He pulled the black sweat shirt on over his head, hiding the art in question. The front of the shirt said ARMY in white block letters, a remnant of his father's career.

"You know I don't allow any of the 'f' words in my house, Jack." My voice elevated. "And you will get a job, soon, if you expect to stay here." His first day home in eight years and already we were back at it. It all felt horribly familiar. And I sounded just like the shrew of a mother I'd been when he was a teen-ager. Even to myself I sounded atrocious.

"I'm sorry. I shouldn't have said that. You must be very hungry. Can I fix you some bacon and eggs, or do you just want to start off with cereal?"

"Naw, I'll fix myself something. You got any steak?"

I knew I had to escape or I'd kill him. "You'll have to look in the refrigerator," I said. "I have a bunch of errands to do this morning. I should be home around noon. Oh, and read that list I left on the table. If you're going to live here, well, there are some rules."

"Yeah, yeah, take your time." He glanced at the list, snorted, then wadded up the paper and threw it in the direction of the waste basket. "You're nuts, Mom." He opened the refrigerator door and started rummaging. "While you're out you better go to the grocery. I don't see much in here I like. And get some steak!"

MASSANUTTEN REGIONAL LIBRARY

Harrisonburg, VA 22801

It was nearly noon by the time I got home. I struggled through the back door loaded with groceries and yelled for Jack.

"Come help me, Jack! There's more in the car."

When there was no answer I went down the hall to his room, knocked and then pushed the door open. Jack was naked on the bed with an equally naked woman writhing on top of him. I slammed the door shut to cut off the sight. I ran back down the hall and escaped the house, spewing my disgust like venom from a snake. I stood by my car, shaking with fury. I felt as violated as if I had been raped.

It was only minutes before the woman crept out the front door and across the yard to a beat up car I hadn't noticed parked at the curb. "And don't come back!" I shouted, as if there were any chance of that.

Jack leaned out the door; bare-chested over ragged jeans, eyes blazing, his face pale. "Thanks, Mom. Nice, real nice. You're a bitch." His words ended with the slam of the door.

I stood in the carport, arms around myself and waited until I stopped shaking, hoping the neighbors weren't looking out a window. My fury finally abated and I finished unloading the car. Before I put the groceries away I took a pen and paper and printed a note: 'No hookers, no drugs, no drinking, and get a job'. I slipped it under his door. A half hour later he left the house without a word. I watched as he slouched away, head down, hands jammed into the pockets of an old jacket of his dad's. I wondered where he was going. I went into his room and stripped the bed.

***

The black dog slinked out of the trees and sniffed around in the clearing, pulling a broken chain behind him. I tried to make myself invisible behind a stand of tall weeds. He ranged across the field as if hunting quail, tail high, head down. Suddenly he stopped, raised his head and looked in my direction. The chain rattled as he leapt toward me, tail down, body flat out, snarling, his sharp teeth dripping saliva. The weeds tangled around me, holding me fast. I had to run…run…run… I woke up in a sweat and shoved the covers away.

Chapter 3

A black limousine from the Tyree Brothers funeral home pulled up in front of the Midsouth City Museum of Fine Art and disgorged seven black, obviously pregnant teenagers. There seemed to be a cosmic drawing of breath as pedestrians paused and drivers slowed and stared. Then as if released from their thrall they either frowned or smiled and went on their way. Meeting them at the curb I greeted the girls and quickly snapped their picture standing with the uniformed driver beside the limo. They turned as one to stare at the building before them and their awe was obvious. It was patterned after the New York Metropolitan Museum of Fine Art with broad steps and handsome columns guarding the doors.

"That the museum?" "We goin' in there?" "Holy ..." Their eyes and mouths were wide open. A few of the girls were dressed in fancy church outfits, for although they lived in the projects they spent Sundays praising God with vigor in churches where the services were lively and the sermons rich with hellfire and damnation. It was clear that all the girls had made an effort to dress in their best.

Kenisha edged over close to me. "This is Tasha," she said, pulling her friend with her, the same girl who had stood laughing at me from the store front window. "This here's my friend Miz Fischer," she said to Tasha, cutting her eyes at me to see if I was going to disagree.

"Hey, Tasha. Nice to see you...again." I smiled at her to let her know there were no hard feelings. "Let's go in, shall we?"

As if unfrozen, the girls began laughing and shoving each other and clambering up the steps. Myra met us just inside the doors. "Come with me, everyone. I need to talk to you before we start our tour." The woman at the information desk set in the middle of the large rotunda smiled as the museum newcomers oh'd and ah'd their way through totally unfamiliar territory. The girls crowded into the cloak room with Myra, still giggling and nudging each other. They put their coats on hangers, hung them on the racks, then gathered around her.

"Have any of you ever been to a museum before?"

A united chorus of "No, ma'am's" was the response.

"OK, then. A museum is like a library. You've all been to the library, haven't you?" Most of the girls nodded. "And what's the big rule in a library?"

Someone timidly suggested, "Be quiet?"

Kenisha whispered sarcastically to Tasha, "No, it's laugh and shout." Tasha giggled. Kenisha performed a little dance step, jostling the girl on her other side who pushed her back.

"Yes, good!" said Myra, ignoring the disruption. "We want to show that we have good manners by being quiet and acting like young ladies."

Unnoticed by the girls, an attractive young woman entered the room and stood at the back. She wore a navy blazer with the museum logo on the upper pocket over a khaki skirt and white blouse.

Myra went on, "And now I want to introduce you to our docent who will be showing us around today. This is Tamika Tolliver."

As the docent worked her way to the front, Kenisha asked, "Miz Boutwell, what did you say she is? A donut?" The girls convulsed.

Oh, boy, what a long day this is going to be, I thought. My eyes met Myra's, confirming that she thought so, too.

Tamika Tolliver took over. "Hey, it does sounds like donut, sort of, doesn't it? No, it's docent. Say it with me. Docent. Do you know what it means?"

The girls mumbled, "No, Ma'am."

"It's just a fancy word for tour guide. In museums and big churches it's what they call people like me. It means that I have studied the things that are in this museum so I can tell people about them. It also means that I know where the restrooms are and that makes me a very important person to have around." She and the girls laughed together.

"Now follow me, and we will begin this adventure. And it is an adventure because you'll see things today that you can't see anyplace else in the world. You'll see what famous artists have done. Not just pictures of their work, but the actual work itself. Who knows a famous artist's name?"

Like the Pied Piper, Tamika led the group out of the cloak room and into the first large gallery. Kenisha, following on her heels said, "Saw a book at school 'bout a guy named Van Gogh. Fool cut his ear off."

Amid the resulting burst of gasps and 'eeuuus', Tamika looked over her shoulder and said, "Good! Excellent! What's your name?"

Kenisha told her, and Tamika went on, "Well, Kenisha, we just happen to have one of Van Gogh's paintings here. Come look."

Seven pregnant teens stepped into a world of paintings and sculpture from the old masters with no idea what they were looking at. Tamika patiently told about ones she especially selected for them to see, keeping it simple and injecting humor as they went along. Often she paused at a bench to let them rest their swollen bodies, and changing the focus, she asked them about themselves. Two of the girls, Tasha and Aretha, shyly admitted that they liked to draw and dreamed of becoming real artists one day. They beamed when Tamika exclaimed, "That's wonderful! Good for you."

Myra and I trailed behind the group. "Wow, she's terrific," I said. "Aren't we lucky to get her?"

"Oh, it's no accident," Myra replied. "Tamika came through the agency herself a few years ago. She's my shining example of what is possible for these girls. She is terrific."

By the time our group gathered for lunch in the museum's food hall where a special table was set for us, Tamika had charmed them completely. Our preordered lunch was served from two large trays by white coated wait staff, and the girls examined their soup and sandwiches suspiciously. Then satisfied that the hamburgers and tomato soup were just like those they got at home, they watched closely as Tamika ate her lunch, mimicking her manners and her mannerisms. Sitting among them, Myra and I quizzed the teens on what they had seen and learned that morning. It was apparent that the tour was a success.

"Did Tamika tell you where she used to live?" asked Myra.

"No," they chorused and turned to look at their new idol.

"I grew up in the Roosevelt project. That's where y'all live, right? I met Mz. Boutwell the same place you did."

Seven mouths dropped open.

"You had a baby, too?" asked one of the girls.

"Yes." Tamika nodded.

"A boy or a girl?"

"A girl."

"Where is she now?" Kenisha asked.

"I gave her up for adoption to a wonderful family who can take better care of her than I could when I was just 15."

Hearing the words, I was sure Tamika had made a terrible error. A chill settled over the table, and as if the adults had vaporized, manners disappeared, and the well-behaved teen-agers morphed into an unruly bunch of little children.

Stubbornly and loudly, Kenisha spoke up for the group. "Not us. We'uns ain't giving up our babies." Six voices joined hers. "That's right." "Nobody gets my baby 'cept me." "Yeah, me, too."

Heads turned and eyes stared in our direction from other diners in the food hall. I frowned at Kenisha and shook my head.

Quickly recovering, Tamika said, "That's OK." She lowered her voice and the girls got quiet in order to hear her. "You don't have to give up your babies. Everyone has to make that choice for themselves. It's just that, for me, it was the choice I made so I could stay in school. I don't know about you, but I wanted out of Roosevelt, and I thought that was the only way I could do it."

A cloud of silence settled over the table as chocolate ice cream was devoured. After a few minutes Tasha spoke up. "I'd like to get out of Roosevelt, too. But I won't give up my baby. My mother gave me up. Just walked out. My grandma takes care of me and my sisters. I don't want my baby to be abandoned, like we was. No way." The others nodded their agreement.

Myra cleared her throat to get their attention. "That's what my job is about, you know. I want to help you all make the right decision for yourselves. And help you make your choice, whatever it is, provide a better life for both you and your babies."

She stood up. "Next week we're going to visit a vocational school, where you'll see some different kinds of jobs that are out there. Maybe some of you will see something that you'd like to learn how to do. Now let's thank Tamika for our nice day and then we'll meet your ride out front."

Myra paid the bill while I herded the girls between tables of curious onlookers toward the front door. I was aghast when I overheard Kenisha in the lobby confronting Tamika.

"You shouldn't have give up your baby, you know. That baby can only love you, and you the only one can love her like a real mother. I ain't givin' up my baby!" She stomped toward the door. Tamika looked shaken.

I hurried over and squeezed her shoulder. "I'm so sorry, Tamika. Kenisha really has a thing about keeping her baby. But she shouldn't have spoken to you like that."

"She can't know what a hard decision that was for me," Tamika said. "I still wonder sometimes if it was right. But I do know that my life and the life of my little girl are better now than they would have been if I had kept her."

Myra walked up, oblivious to the little drama she'd just missed. "Thanks to both of you for what you did today. Hopefully this will be the beginning of a look at the outside world that will help these girls see beyond the projects. Come on Roberta, let's get these kids back in the limo and headed home. Thanks again, Tamika. I'll be talking with you soon."

When we reached the curb the limo was just pulling up. I snatched Kenisha by her sleeve and pulled her away from the other girls. "I can't believe you spoke to Tamika like that. That was just rude. She's hurt, you know, and you have no right to judge her."

"Ain't givin' up my baby."

"Yes, well that's for you to decide. Tamika decided what was best for her, and that's her right. Do you understand?"

"I guess. I gotta go." She pulled away from me and went to get in the limo. She didn't look back.

On Monday I was surprised when Kenisha came into the agency and walked directly to my desk, flopping down in the side chair. She had on the same clothes she'd worn on Saturday, rumpled now and spotted with something unsavory-looking on her blouse. "I wanna ast you something. Did that Tamika lady really grow up in Roosevelt?"

"Yes, she did. Why do you ask?"

"How far did she get in school, I mean, did she get to college and all that?"

"Yes, she's in college now and works as a docent when she doesn't have classes. I think she's going to become a teacher after she graduates in June."

Kenisha seemed to change the subject. "When I got home Saturday? My momma was passed out on the couch. All them kids was crying and fussin' and there wasn't nothing in the place to eat. It was a mess." She looked at me with tears in her eyes. "I called my aunt and she come over to help. I don't know what we're gonna do, though."

"I'm sure Myra and social services will work something out. You're going to talk to her now, aren't you?"

Kenisha nodded, still sniffling. I handed her a tissue from a box in the desk drawer.

"You'd rather be like Tamika, I guess. I know she's had to work hard to get this far. But she's stubborn, like you, and I'm sure she'll make it. I'd like to help you make it, too, you know."

"But I ain't giving up my baby!" Kenisha wore her determination like a bullet proof vest.

"I know. I know. Tell you what. Would you go to the mall with me on Saturday? I'd like to get something for your baby. And we could have lunch."

"Maybe. Might not be able to get out, you know?"

"Well, let's try for it, anyway. Call me, OK?" I gave her my number. I dared to hope that I might make a difference in this kid's life, starting Saturday.

Chapter 4

It didn't take me long to realize that Jack needed some decent clothes in order to look for a job. When he brought it up, I think I surprised him with my quick response.

"OK, let's go to Wal-Mart and get what you need."

"Really?" He looked astonished. "Now?"

I felt a little astonished myself but I could hardly promise Kenisha that I'd go shopping with her without doing at least as much for my own son.

"Really. Now." I put on my coat and took the car keys. In a minute he joined me looking pleased and excited.

On the way we made a list. Underwear, socks, jeans, shirts, sweaters or sweats, warm coat. Oh, and shoes. By the time we drove into the huge parking lot we were ready. Jack leapt from the car and took off like a shot. When I found him inside the store in the men's section I admonished, "Don't go hog wild now," and then lurked nearby while Jack pawed through the stacks of jeans and shirts. I assumed he didn't want or need my advice on his selections.

Not many shoppers were out that weekday morning. I did notice one short, very portly woman near me wearing a tan, tent-like, all weather coat. Remember Columbo? Like that. She too was looking at cardigans, taking them off the rack and holding them up for inspection. She looked longingly at a particularly bright red one. In the aisle pairs of Seniors paced by on their morning exercise routes, their Nikes squeaking out a cadence on the rubber runner while their elbows pumped rhythmically. Their faces all wore a serious, determined look.

"Hey Mom, come here." Even after eight years that voice spoke directly to something deep inside me. A couple of days at home with a good bed, quiet nights (a rarity in jails he had told me), and lots of food, Jack was losing that haunted prison look and sounded almost cheerful. He was clean shaven except for a neatly trimmed mustache that I hadn't even noticed the night he came home.

I made my way out of the women's department and across the aisle. "Need some help?" I asked.

"Yeah, I need to try on these pants. Watch my cart, will you?"

While I waited I looked through his selections. He'd done well...except for one quite expensive black leather jacket I found at the bottom of the stack, looking suspiciously as if it were tucked there on purpose.

"What do you think?" Jack stood in the three-way mirror, turning to check out the rear view.

"Well, jeans are jeans. How do they feel?" Whatever happened to nice slacks with cuffs and creases, I wondered.

His look of disgust told me that was not the fashionista response he was hoping for. I recalled that Jack's usual fashion statement had been of the 'Dapper Dan meets Joe Sixpack' variety. He disappeared into the dressing room again and returned modeling yet another pair of jeans. This time he didn't ask my opinion.

We moved on to the underwear and socks section where I sank onto a chair next to a tall, skinny, weather-wrinkled man almost hidden in the folds of a puffy brown jacket.

He wore muddy work boots, and held a fur-lined cap in hands that told a history of hard work on rough jobs.

"Ah, feels good to sit." I said. "I'm waiting for my son."

"Wife," he grunted. "Wore out her old long underwear. She shows me a bunch of holes, I say, 'well hell woman get some new'. So here we are." He looked at the clock on a far wall. "I gotta get back to work. MARJEAN!"

His shout brought my fellow cardigan shopper scurrying from the walls of bundled socks and underwear. A bright red sweater hung across one arm while the other held several soft bundles. He rose to meet her, gave me a curt nod, and led poor Marjean off to check out. From the rear they looked a bit like Mutt and Jeff, or Tom and Jerry. But not funny.

I utilized the vacant chair to sort Jack's things. Pants (both pairs of jeans), shirts, sweaters, sweats. All those I put back in the cart. The expensive jacket I kept on my lap. When he appeared carrying a few white bundles of his own, we took stock. He still needed shoes.

"And we need to discuss this jacket," I said. "I'll pay for a warm coat for every day, but this leather jacket is something you can buy for yourself when you get a job. I know it's handsome, but it isn't warm, and it's very expensive."

His light, "Can't get anything past you, can I, Ma?" surprised me. He was being unusually pleasant, but then I was being unusually generous. Wasn't I?

"I'll put it back on the rack and get a coat. Come on. Bring the cart."

He took the jacket and headed back to the outer garments section with me trailing behind. I watched as he returned the leather jacket to the rack and then I helped him make a wiser choice. After that it was off to get some shoes. Good grief, do you know how much Adidas cost? I wrote it off as the price for quenching a guilty conscience and showing what a loving mother I could be.

We finally finished his shopping and I left him to go and pick up a few things for myself. I always hated to shop and did it as rarely as possible. A few minutes later I met Jack at the checkout line. He went first and explained to the clerk that I would be paying for his purchases as well as the ones in the basket I was holding. I smiled and waved my credit card at the lady. In front of me Jack hovered over the counter, effectively blocking my view, although I didn't think anything of it at the moment. I was content to ponder the choice of chewing gum or Chiclets on the rack beside me.

"Do you want these separate or together?" The clerk paused as she finished checking Jack's purchases. Jack was being helpful by bagging his own things and putting them in the cart.

Jack interrupted. "Gimme the keys and I'll go put these in the car and get it warmed up."

I handed him the keys and told the clerk, "Oh, together will be OK, I guess."

The man in line behind me seemed in a great rush, so I crushed the long receipt into my pocket without looking at it, grabbed my parcel from the clerk and went out to the car. I made Jack get out of the driver's seat and go around to the other side. Before I fastened my seat belt I pulled the store receipt from my pocket and glanced at the total.

In a burst of words Jack said, "Come on, hurry up. I wanta get home and try on my new things. And thanks a lot, Mom. I really appreciate this. I know I'll..." He jabbered on.

I'd ceased to hear what Jack was saying. The total on the receipt took my breath away and when I checked the individual items, I couldn't believe what I was seeing.

I turned in my seat to confront him.

"You got the jacket anyway." My voice was low, quivering. My eyes squinted into his, sending a searing message.

"Oh, come on, Mom. I been stuck in that goddam prison for eight years. It's the least you can do. I deserve something decent to wear. You try living in a fucking orange monkey suit all day every day and see how it makes you feel."

"Get it."

"What?"

"I said 'get it'. Now." My voice rose two notes. It was no longer quivering.

Jack opened the door and stepped out. He leaned in and said, "You're a fuckin' bitch, old lady. You hear me? A fuckin' bitch!" He slammed the door and stalked away. It had started to snow again, and I watched him disappear across the parking lot.

I got out of the car and opened the trunk. I found the leather jacket and took it back into the store. At the returns counter I explained, "There was a mistake. I want to return this jacket." Marjean's husband stood at the counter near me. He was returning a pretty, bright red sweater. I looked around but didn't see Marjean.

When Jack came home later that day an uneasy truce settled between us. The leather jacket was never mentioned, but he looked nice in his new clothes and even managed to thank me again.

Life with Jack settled into a pattern. He never ate with me, but raided the refrigerator and fixed his own meals or ate my leftovers. He did his own laundry, but left his bathroom a soggy mess. I found it was better for me if I cleaned it up myself rather than let my anger burn when he didn't do it. When he left the house in the mornings he'd tell me he was applying for jobs around the city.

"They don't want to hire a convicted felon," Jack whined one day when I discovered him lying on his bed around noon.   "Well, you won't find anything lying here. Keep looking. I'm sure you'll locate something soon. Maybe you can find some sidewalks to shovel in the meantime. At least that would give you some spending money." He'd been "borrowing" from me, and where it went I didn't know. I was sure it wasn't coming back.

He spent the rest of the day lolling about, watching TV, snacking from the cupboard and refrigerator, or standing at my shoulder watching me do my various chores. He acted like he did just before he started kindergarten.

"What if I can't get a job? I can't help it if no one will hire me." His whimper was piteous. "You won't kick me out, will you? Please, Mom." I thought he might cry.

"No, I won't kick you out. But you'll get a job. You just have to get out there and keep looking." I tried to sound upbeat. I was relieved when he finally went to bed.

The next day I showered and was dressing when Jack passed my door and called, "See you later!" He sounded cheerful. It was only when I checked my wallet to see if I had enough money for my errands and the luncheon I was going to that I felt slapped across the face. The one hundred dollar bill I kept in the secret compartment of my purse was gone.

My anger blazed like a fire splashed with kerosene. It frightened me. It always did. I cursed and screamed with my mouth shut so the neighbors wouldn't hear. I pounded my fists on the wall and kicked a door. And finally, I cried.

I ditched my plans for errands and the ladies luncheon, and hurried to a small church nearby where my Al-

Anon group met three times a week. I got there just as the gathering of 15 men and women begin saying in unison, "Lord, grant me the serenity to accept the things I cannot change, courage to change the things I can, and the wisdom to know the difference. Amen." If I had learned nothing else in these rooms, that was wisdom enough. It took me months to understand and accept that you can change yourself, but you can't change other people. It was a hard lesson but I had plenty of opportunities to practice its wisdom. As in all Al-Anon groups, the reading of the Twelve Steps followed. "We admitted we were powerless over alcohol – that our lives had become unmanageable. Came to believe that a Power greater than ourselves could restore us to sanity. Made a decision to turn our will and our lives over to the care of God *as we understood Him*. Made a searching and fearless inventory of ourselves."

As the reading went on I realized that I was back at square one with Jack home again.

"We're glad to see you back, Roberta," the leader said. No last names were ever used. Twelve Step programs emphasize anonymity.

"Thanks, everyone. I'll be here more often now. Jack came home last week. I'm going to need your help." Friendly murmurs around the table reassured me of their constant support.

"The lesson today is 'anger'," the leader announced. "Roberta, how about reading today's page?"

I marveled at how often the lesson was precisely what I needed. The lesson ended with a quote from the book *'One Day at a Time in Al-Anon'*. "No one can control the insidious effect of alcohol, or its power to destroy the graces and decencies of life…But we do have a power, derived from God, and that is the power to change our own lives."

I sat in my car in the parking lot after the Al-Anon meeting. The winter sun warmed the car and it felt good. I didn't want to go home, and it was too late to go to the luncheon I'd made plans for. A tap on the window startled me. Dan, also coming from the meeting, motioned me to roll down my window. "Did you hear that the Japanese have lost a man in space?" he asked.

"Oh, no!" I was shocked at the thought.

"Yes, they say there's a nip in the air." Dan was grinning from ear to ear.

"Oh, you goofball. That's not nice." I hated that I bit so hard on his corny joke, and more than a little dismayed at how offensive it was. But he seemed to be a nice guy, a retired teacher. His daughter worked at our camp one summer. I didn't know he also had a son until he talked about Mike in the meetings.

"Will you join me for lunch?" he asked. "I know a place where the salads are good, and they have great barbeque. Or better yet, a bowl of good hot soup on a day as cold as this. I can recommend their white chili. My treat."

"Oh. Well, I don't know." I looked at the man. A big guy, he wore his white hair cropped short and his matching beard well-trimmed. Black eyebrows topped hazel eyes. I knew about his daughter and son. I didn't know anything about a wife. I was positive I hadn't cared for his politically incorrect gag.

Dan smiled, showing perfect white teeth, and I caved. "Sure, why not?"

He got in the car and gave directions to Max's Chili Bowl, a few blocks away. When we arrived Dan took my coat and hung it on the rack while I settled myself and looked at the menu. We agreed on the white chili and he ordered for both of us.

While we waited for our food we talked about the group and danced around a little about our own personal stuff. I found out he was divorced. I only fudged a little about my age and said I'd been divorced for a long time. Talking with Dan was easy, I learned. Just pop in a question now and then, and sit back. When the waitress brought our order I found that I liked the chili, the first white chili I'd ever eaten. We ate in silence for a few minutes.

We started talking then about the one thing we had in common. Our sons. Both had gotten off the track, somehow. Dan's son was in jail, but would be out soon.

"And your Jack just got home. Is he OK?" Dan had finished his chili, pushed back from the table and was sipping a cup of hot tea.

"I don't really know, yet." I told him about the call girl I discovered in his bed and my explosive reaction.

"It's just so disgusting that he would do that in my house," I said through gritted teeth, the bile rising in my throat.

"Now, come on, Roberta, he's a grown man who has been in prison for the past seven years. He does have needs, you know. It's natural. No doubt he chose the wrong time and place to do it, but your anger seems a bit over the top, don't you think?" His face showed concern, but there was amusement in his eyes.

Well, men. What do you expect? "I suppose so," I said. Then, "It's getting late, I've got to go. Thanks for lunch and for listening to my sad story. I'm usually a lot more fun."

"Wait. You need to take me back to the church to get my car."

"Oh, yeah, I forgot." No quick escape after all.

We bundled into our coats, hats, and gloves. Dan went to pay the bill and we drove back to the church with little conversation.

"See you next week," he said, getting out of the car.

"See you, and thanks again."

As I drove away I pondered his remark about my anger being a bit 'over the top'. Easy for him to say. And what about his tasteless joke? Oh, well. Nice eyes, though.

***

I dreaded the fight Jack and I would have about the $100 he took from my wallet that morning so I was pleasantly surprised when I got home and saw that the walks and driveway were shoveled clean. Howard was shoveling his driveway. Maybe he did mine, too. I waved. He waved back. I could see a light in the kitchen as I pulled in and parked.

"I got a job!" Jack greeted me as I stepped in the door. "I was just walking past this place and something told me to go in and ask. So I did and they hired me." He closed the refrigerator with his hip, his hands full.

"What kind of place? What kind of job?" I pushed aside the thought of confronting him about the $100....for the time being.

"It's a builders' supply store. They sell lumber and everything else it takes to build any kind of building. At first I'll just be helping out wherever they need me. Then they said they'd see, and they'd assign me a regular job of my own." Jack stacked turkey slices on whole wheat bread slathered with mayo and mustard. His eyes sparkled. "I cleaned off the sidewalk and the driveway. Did you notice?"

"Yes, I did. Thank you. When do you start?"

"Tomorrow. I have to be there by 7:30 so I'll have to get up really early. It's two miles, so I'll have to leave about 6:30. It's a pretty long walk, but I can do it. I'm going to need some new shoes, boots with steel toes, they said."

I grabbed the opening. "You can get them out of the $100 you took from my wallet this morning, and then pay me back when you get paid. You cannot live here and steal from me, Jack. I won't have it."

He looked slightly chastened, and did not deny the theft.

"OK, I will, but I won't get paid for two weeks. It's just minimum wage to start but they'll give me a raise in about six weeks if I do OK. They are real nice. The guy that interviewed me took me around and introduced me to everyone. One old guy has worked there for 30 years."

He chattered on like he did his first day home from kindergarten. It pleased me to see him so happy and excited. His melancholy was gone, and somehow the $100 faded in importance from my mind.

Jack seemed happy for the first time since he got home, and I gave him a hug. "I'm happy for you, Jack. Good going."

I went next door for a few minutes to visit with Howard as he finished up his snow removal task. He was a good neighbor and I wanted to tell him about Jack. But first we had to discuss our bird feeders, and what kinds of birds we were attracting. We had an unannounced contest going and we kept our choice of bird foods secret.

"I notice you're getting a lot more cardinals, now. What are you using?" I asked.

"Yeah, I changed brands this last time. I forget the name." Enigmatic is the word that came to my mind for the look on his face.

"I'm looking to get more woodpeckers and nuthatches. I have a new recipe to put in my suet feeder," I countered, but with no offer to share it.

We grinned at each other, knowing we had each scored a point. We were comfortable neighbors, Howard and I. Actually, Howard was a great neighbor. Everyone up and down the street knew him because he was willing to lend a hand whenever a hand was needed. Once I mentioned I needed a small bench to fit under the windows in my living room. He took measurements and built one for me in his workshop out back. And one day when I was trying to use muriatic acid to remove some white paint from the red bricks of my house, he brought over a can of brick red paint and said, "Here use this. It's easier, and a whole lot faster."

I balanced his good deeds by occasionally sharing some baked goods or by picking up his mail when he was away visiting his children for a few days.

"I guess you've noticed that Jack is home. The good news is that he just got a job...finally."

"Yeah, he told me when we were out here cleaning off our sidewalks. Good for him. It sounds great. I know you're relieved."

We chatted some more then I went back to my house. The thing about Howard was that I never felt I got beyond the surface with him. He always held back, and I sometimes wondered what he was hiding, or hiding from.

Chapter 5

Kenisha was standing on the corner of Lincoln and Martin Luther King Drive where I picked her up. She was wrapped in a worn tan coat with fake fur trim, her head was bare and her legs were sporting colorful striped stockings above her scruffy boots.

"Whooee! It's cold out there," She got in and slammed the door.

"Good morning." The heater was turned on high and I turned it back to medium when she got settled with a seatbelt on. "It'll be a good day to be inside the mall. How are you doing?"

"I'm OK. They come and got the little kids, though. I don't like that. Momma's gotta go to rehab when they get a space for her they say. Then it'll be just me and Jerome and Calvin.

"How old are Jerome and Calvin?"

"Jerome's 16 and goes to high school. He's real smart and a good basketball player. He's hoping for a college scholarship. Calvin is 17. He just sort of, uh, hangs around."

The parking lot at Riverside Mall had many open spaces, and I got one as close to a door as I could. Kenisha and I rushed around huge piles of plowed snow to get inside quickly.

"I could use a cup of something hot, couldn't you?" I asked, heading for the food court.

Like all malls, it echoed with the sound of many voices, and Kenisha's head spun like a top to take in everything she could. She headed straight to a window where teen fashions were on display. "Oh, Mz. Fischer, look at this."

Before I could get there she dashed to another and was calling, "Mz. Fischer. Come look." A model kitchen in a home store was the attraction. "That stove is funny. See, the top is just flat. How does that work? Can we go inside and look?"

A salesman lurked close by as the gray-haired white lady and the pregnant black teenager toured his kitchen and exclaimed at all its wonders. Finally relenting he joined us and explained the machine that just makes ice, and the advantages of the amazingly futuristic flat top stove. Kenisha fell in love with them and the side by side refrigerator/freezer that spurted ice and water from its door. "Ain't nothin' like this anyplace in Roosevelt," she said wistfully.

"Ain't nothin' like it at my house, either," I echoed. "Come on, let's go get something hot to drink. Thanks for helping us," I said to the salesman. "We'll be back....in about 10 years." He smiled gamely.

"I hope you will," he said, "and remember to ask for me: Wilbur." He winked.

We all laughed, then Kenisha and I headed for the food court where I got a cup of mocha latte and she got some cocoa and a muffin. Settled at a table we watched the people go by. Our silence was comfortable. Kenisha shed her heavy coat and leaned over the table to eat the crumbly muffin. She took a sip of cocoa and sat back.

"My momma would never have been nice to that salesman. He didn't really want us in there, you know. Or at least he didn't want me." Her black eyes were somber in her open young face.

I thought about that for a while. "I expect he knew we weren't going to buy anything. But when we acted nice he decided to act nice, too. It often works that way." I backed away from confronting the obvious, the racial issue. Kenisha ducked her head and finished the muffin. She didn't say anything.

We cleared off the table, put our trash in the bin, and headed down the mall. At a kiosk Kenisha tried on several winter hats ending with a wildly colored fleece fedora. Her pixie face beamed from under the brim.

"You need a hat. Let's buy it." I opened my purse and offered a bill to the attendant.

"Really?" Kenisha asked. She looked at herself in the little mirror. Her delight was almost heartbreaking.

"OK, now let's go find something for that baby," I said. "Do you know if it's a boy or a girl?"

"She's a girl." But before we left the kiosk Kenisha turned to the attendant. "Thanks for your help," she said.

"My pleasure," the young Hispanic woman smiled back.

We skipped the 'Grandma's Darlin' Boutique'and headed to Pennys where I knew there would be lots to choose from in a price range I could afford. For an hour Kenisha reverently paged through the racks of dresses. Each outfit was cuter than the other. She gazed at the packaged knit snuggly things, and tinkered with the colorful teething toys hanging from a hook. Finally she made up her mind; a ruffly knit dress in pink plaid with matching panties. I added a few of the knit snugglies for practical purposes.

"A good choice," I told her as the clerk rang up the pink dress. "She will look adorable in that. Why don't you pick out a little toy for her, too? Every kid needs a toy."

I was exhausted. Almost two hours of shopping had done me in. "Ready for lunch?" I asked Kenisha.

"Yes ma'am. I could eat a pig." A happier little pregnant girl you would never see and I felt happy, too.

We strolled along discussing our choices of places to eat, when a trio of mean-looking 'gangbangers' moved into our path. Kenisha clutched her packages to her chest and in a low voice cursed. Alarmed, I closed the space between us.

"What's the matter?" I spoke to her, but my eyes never left the hooligans.

"Yo, l'il momma! Wha' cha' doin'?" The three young black men strutted nearer. With do-rags and baseball caps on sideways, baggy pants almost falling off their hips, and Nikes without laces on their feet, they were a shopkeeper's worst nightmare. Mine, too, truth be told.

"Cha' got there?" One of the boys grabbed at Kenisha's parcels. Expertly she turned her shoulder to him, and hugged the packages tightly with both arms. The other boys crowded closer.

"Now just a minute," I warned, reaching an arm across in front of Kenisha.

"Fuck off, Calvin!"

Startled, I realized we were in Kenisha's world now

"This your rich honky friend?" Calvin smirked at me, still grabbing for the packages.

"Damn it, Calvin! Leave me alone! Get away." Kenisha showed no fear. Her eyes sparked anger, though. One of the other boys circled behind Kenisha and snatched her new hat. Unnoticed I removed my collapsible cane from its carrying loops on the side of my shoulder bag and spun toward him.

With my most commanding shout, "HeeYaa!" I lunged into my best T'ai Chi attack stance, snapping the cane to its full length. I jabbed it into his stomach. He doubled over, flipping the hat into the air and grabbing my cane, jerking it out of my hand. I didn't quite catch the obviously vile name he called me.

Just then Kenisha stomped down hard, her boot heel having telling effect on Calvin's canvas-clad foot. At the same time she swung around and confronted his buddies. "I said 'Back off', Bobby and James, and I mean it. Jerome will be coming to see you if you don't leave us alone."

"Ow! You little bitch," Calvin howled as he backed away and signaled his friends to back off, too. "I'll see you at home," he snarled. My opponent, Bobby, it seems, reluctantly shuffled into reverse, slinging my cane down the shiny floor of the mall.

I was greatly relieved to see Calvin and his friends slouch away, laughing loudly and making rude comments laced with obscenities. Calvin was limping and Bobby seemed to be holding his stomach. A security guard came from a side hall and shadowed them. Soon another guard joined him. They turned a corner and we couldn't see them anymore .

We had attracted a small crowd. Moving from the cover of store front doorways they approached us and a smattering of applause broke out. One young teenager handed Kenisha her hat. "That was awesome," she said.

A man picked up my cane and brought it to me, asking, "Did you lose this?" I thanked him, then bowed to the audience.

"Thank you, thank you," I said, and took Kenisha by the arm.

We left our admirers, chose a restaurant instead of the food court for lunch, and settled into a dark booth. A giggle started low and slow in my belly and worked its way up until it burst forth. Kenisha started, too, and soon we were both laughing hysterically

"You were awesome," I said to Kenisha, as I tried to catch my breath.

"You, too, Mz. Fischer." She raised her hand, palm out, and we joined in my first ever "high-five", and laughed some more.

Kenisha had a basket of riblets while I settled for a fish sandwich. We ate for a while and finally I said, "So that's Calvin?"

"Yeah. He's a dumb ass." Looking embarrassed she added, "Sorry."

"Are you afraid to go home?"

"No, he's just showing off for the "bro's". He'll be OK at home. He knows Jerome'll kill him if he does anything to me."

She looked as if she hoped this were true. I sat there wondering how I could bring up the subject of her future, when Kenisha put down her fork and look intently at me.

"Why are you being nice to me?"

Taken aback, I sat there and pondered the question. Finally I admitted, "I'm not sure myself, Kenisha. I just feel like something clicked between us right from that first day when you conned me out of ten bucks. Crazy, huh?"

She rejected my answer with a shake of her head, and returned to her ribs. I tried again.

"Okay. Maybe this is the answer. I have a son who is almost 50 years old. He just got out of prison for the umpteenth time and is at home living with me. He finally got a job just the other day making minimum wage. When I met you, a smart and yes, cute, young girl who could probably be anything she wants to be, I just felt like maybe this is my second chance to help a kid turn out OK."

I didn't like the way that sounded, so I took another stab at it. "I'm sorry, I know you're going to turn out OK no matter what I do. I just would like to hope that maybe together we could make your future be something even better." As an afterthought I added, "And something that would make your mother and Jerome proud of you, too. Lame as it sounds, I just want to help."

"What's your boy's name?" Kenisha asked.

"Jack."

"Is he your only one?"

"Yes."

"You didn't have any more?"

I stopped short of explaining about adopting Jack. "No. Just the one."

Kenisha looked thoughtful for a few minutes. "OK."

"OK?"

That's all. Just "OK". We had a deal! I love a challenge.

***

Smokey's was crowded and noisy but Myra and I managed to find a table toward the back. In a chic gray pant suit over a purple turtle neck sweater she looked stylish, as usual.

After we ordered, I filled her in on my adventure with Kenisha at the Mall over the weekend.

"You should have seen little pregnant Kenisha. She was magnificent."

Myra smiled but then freaked when I happened to mention my small part in the little drama.

"You did what?" she shrieked. The people at the next table turned and stared. She lowered her voice. "You could have been hurt! I thought your T'ai Chi classes were just an exercise thing."

"Well, they are, but they also are a little bit of martial arts, too." I waved aside her angst and voiced my graver concern. "Will they leave her in that apartment alone with two brothers when her mother goes to rehab? Even if Kenisha isn't afraid of Calvin, I'm afraid for her." I wiped the sauce off my face and picked up another rib. Kenisha's had looked good at the Mall.

Myra sipped her tea. "I'll make sure her case manager knows about the incident at the Mall. You're right, it's dangerous to have her there with just the two boys. I expect when Social Services hears about this, they will make some other arrangements for her."

Relieved, I went on to tell her that Kenisha and I agreed that I could help her, even if we don't know exactly what that means, yet. "I hope this is OK with you, Myra. I'm not trying to do your job, just maybe put a little frosting on the cake for Kenisha."

"No, that's great. I'm limited in what I can do. We're going to the Vo-Tech school next week. Maybe you can talk with her afterwards and help her see the possibilities. Her home life stinks, but if she thinks there's someone like you she can depend on maybe it will help her make wise decisions…we can hope." She paused, then added, "Just be sure you realize you're making a commitment you can't take lightly."

Back at the office my head churned with thoughts for Kenisha's future. It didn't occur to me that if Al-Anon teaches that you can't change other people it applied to Kenisha just as much as to Jack. Seems that in life you're always on a learning curve.

Chapter 6

On Tuesday I was again at the little Lutheran church for the Al-Anon meeting. I got there early as it was my turn to set up the room and put out the materials and books. Dan skidded in almost on the hour and came to sit next to me. There was no time for chit-chat as the leader started the meeting right on time. The discussion was about 'gratitude' and I shared that Jack finally started a new job.

"Talk about gratitude! I'm thrilled," I concluded. The friendly faces around the table smiled and nodded. They are there for you when the news is good, as well as when it is bad. It was also my turn to straighten the room after the meeting, and Dan hung around to help. He suggested lunch again.

"I'd like to ask what you think I should do about Mike."

I hesitated, but being asked for advice is too flattering an opportunity to turn down.

"Well, OK, but I'll pay my own way." I had no interest in what they call a 'relationship' these days and wanted him to know it.

"Of course," he said. He straightened the chairs while I locked up the book cabinet. This time we drove our own cars to the chili place.

Talk about his son he did. It seemed as if he'd had a pretty normal childhood. At least he'd finished high school. "Mike was a great soccer player and we drove all over taking him to his games," Dan said. "But then he got into the drug thing and all the good stuff just melted away. His mother and I were heartsick."

"I know that feeling," I said. But what I didn't know was the feeling of being a soccer mom. I'd missed that whole chapter in the 'family rites of passage' book. No band performances, no athletic events, no school plays. Just calls from the principal or visits from the police.

"Since your son has already come home, do you have any suggestions for me for when Mike gets released?"

I pondered that for a while. "Dan, I wish I could help, but the truth is I'm doing the 'one day at a time' thing with Jack. Up until he got this new job we were really struggling. Now things are much better, but who knows how long it will last? As I said, 'one day at a time'. That's the best I can do, I'm afraid."

"Well, thanks. I'll keep that in mind." He seemed a bit disappointed that I didn't have a ready recipe for helping released prisoners make a smooth re-entry into society. I wish.

Before I could get away, Dan said, "By the way, the high school is doing 'Oliver' next week and I have tickets. Would you like to go?"

"Well, gosh, OK." My Lord, a date? How many years had it been since I'd had a date? I couldn't remember. Did I mention that he has very long lashes over those amazing hazel eyes?

***

Jack left the house early every morning. It was, he told me, two miles through neighborhoods of small homes with fenced yards, children and dogs, and small corner shops. He walked over some railroad tracks and across to the other side of the main east/west highway through the city to get to his job. The business was a family-owned builder's supply store that had been in business for nearly 40 years. It included both a large hardware store and a full lumber yard. The 'Old Man' was past retirement age but came in nearly every day. His daughter Muriel acted as treasurer of the corporation and with the general manager, oversaw day to day operations. It was a busy place.

Jack loved it. He told me about the different things he had done; putting up stock, waiting on customers, calling a distributor. I was amazed at the variety of things they allowed such a new employee to do.

"They want to try me out at everything until they decide where they want to put me permanently. They like me, Mom." He said that rather wistfully as if it were not a common experience for him.

I noticed, too, that his demeanor was changing. From a shuffling, head down, invisible man, he was morphing into a tall, straight-backed and proud looking citizen. My heart soared.

On Saturday at the CuppaJava with Julie we settled into our habitual window table. It had been a great week for me. Julie was a good listener and I was eager to share.

"Jack loves his job," I reported. "He sets his own alarm and gets up and out of the house without any help from me. So far he hasn't complained about his two-mile jaunt to the store in the cold, and he sits with me at the dinner table every night, and talks! Things seem surprisingly like... dare I say it.... normal."

"That's wonderful, Roberta. Frame it and hang it on the wall." Julie gave me the 'we've been here before, but will it last?' look, and I nodded, knowing that the adage 'one day at a time' was full of truth.

Moving on I told her about Kenisha, leaving out the part about the altercation at the Mall. "She's on a field trip to the vocational school today. I hope she sees something that appeals to her. Anything that will help her out of that cesspool she's living in. I'd like you to meet her sometime…or rather I'd like her to meet you. I think the more different kinds of people she gets to know, the more she'll see the possibilities life has to offer."

"Good idea." Julie nibbled her scone and sipped her latte, her red tennie clad foot bouncing with excess energy. Today her sweat shirt said USC. "We could go visit one of our foster homes and she could play with some of the cats and kittens. Or we could stop by Valley Pet Veterinary Clinic. You know Kate from the SNIP board. She's the director there. They're a great bunch of people."

We kicked around some possible times for doing that, and then I offered, "You know, I think I may have a gentleman friend."

Julie's mouth opened, but nothing came out. Her eyes widened, and she carefully replaced her cup on the table. "Tell, tell!" she finally managed, breaking into a huge grin.

I told her about Dan. "I don't understand it. He's brilliant, and handsome, and seven years younger than I am. I can't imagine what he sees in me. It's a deep mystery, as far as I'm concerned. Or maybe I'm reading too much into it. But we had lunch together twice and he invited me to see a play with him next week."

Being the good friend she is Julie quickly pointed out that I was cute, and smart, and funny. And I reminded her that I was old, a bit chunky, and was losing my memory.

As we parted ways, Julie hugged me and whispered in my ear, "You go, girl."

Driving back to the house I chuckled. Maybe things were going to be OK after all.

Chapter 7

"Please, Mz. Fischer. Could you come? I can't…stop it, Calvin! Stop it! Please, Mz. Fischer, could you come…?"

"I'll be there as soon as I …" The phone went dead. I broke speed records getting to Roosevelt Homes, not knowing what I was going to find. When I got to the project, I had to search for the right address. I could hear the traffic humming up on the interstate. Roosevelt is an unattractive anthill where the city tries to hide its poor. Just a bunch of gray cinderblock buildings, two stories high, liberally decorated with graffiti, they look like old motels complete with outside staircases. When I finally found Kenisha's place it had to be on the second floor, of course. On the steps, I puffed a bit and pulled myself up by the rusty railing. At the top I unsnapped my cane from its loops and whipped it to its full length. Drawing myself to my full five feet four inches I tried to look vigorous and younger by 10 years as I approached apartment 212. Using my cane I rapped loudly.

"Kenisha? Kenisha?" I used my most commanding voice. I heard footsteps, and the door opened a crack. I pushed the door back and stepped into a cave. Blankets covered the windows and a 60 watt bulb in a small lamp with a shade the color of toast cast more shadows than light.

She was standing just inside the door. "Kenisha? Are you OK? Oh, my goodness, honey." Tears streamed down her cheeks, and she was trembling. I didn't see any blood, thank God.

She grabbed my hand. "Oh, Mz. Fischer. Thanks for coming. I…"

"Yo, ol' lady!" Calvin strutted into the room. "You come to rescue my li'l sister? Now, I wouldn't hurt my own li'l sister, would I?" He pulled her away from me and wrapped an arm around her neck, not lovingly.

"I see ya got yer stick, there. Want I should take it away from you?" The smell of liquor was strong on his breath. "I can snap it in two like that." His fingers blasted out one shot after another. "I can snap you in two, too." His laugh sounded manic to me. Oh, why hadn't I had called the police, or Myra?

"OK, that's enough, Calvin. Let her go. She's your sister, and she's pregnant. I know you don't want to hurt her or the baby, so let her go."

"And just what are you goin' to do to make me let her go, old woman? Poke me with your little stick?"

"Just let her go now. This has gone far enough."

Although the room was cold, little waterfalls were tickling down my sides and I could swear my knees were rattling. This felt like the time I was in a canoe trying to catch a young alligator that had invaded our camp lake, and wondering what I would do if I caught it. Kenisha struggled to get out of Calvin's grasp.

The front door crashed open. "I just heard you say 'help', Kenisha. I got here as fast as I could. What's wrong?"

A tall, good looking youth in jeans and a varsity jacket peered into the gloom. Calvin let go of Kenisha and backed away. "Well, hey, J'rome. You home early," he said, his voice slick as olive oil.

Kenisha escaped to Jerome's side. "What's going on?" he asked her. Before she could answer he looked at me. "I'm Jerome, who are you?"

Speechless, my eyes were following Calvin as he tried to slip behind Kenisha and Jerome, toward the door. Without even turning around Jerome reached his arm out and grabbed Calvin by his collar. "You ain't goin' no place, bro."

With Calvin collared, Kenisha spoke up. "He's mad 'cause I stomped him the other day at the Mall. He keeps pokin' an' pokin'. Momma's not here and I couldn't get him to stop. This is Mz. Fischer. I called her, too."

Kenisha stopped crying and came to join me on the derelict sofa where I plopped when my knees failed. "I just want Calvin to leave me alone."

I slipped the telephone off the end table and, holding it in my lap, dialed Myra. Keeping my voice low, I said, "We have a situation here at Kenisha's and I think you need to be here."

"Oh! On my way. Half an hour."

"You leave her alone, you hear me?" Jerome was shaking Calvin by the collar. "Any more shit like this and I'm going to 'accidentally' tip Maurice off to where some of his profits are going. You got that? You got that?" Calvin's teeth rattled as Jerome shook him like a dog with an old sock.

"Yeah, yeah. I was just havin' some fun. Let me go." Calvin twisted away and stumbled to the door. Leaving, he mumbled a stream of curses. My vocabulary was growing exponentially.

By the time Myra arrived Kenisha was calm and Jerome and I were talking basketball. My blood pressure and my knees were back to normal. It was obvious that we needed to get little Miss Kenisha pregnant teeny bopper out of this mess. Jerome and I had agreed and it didn't take us long to convince Myra, too.

"Trouble is, there's no place available to put her tonight," Myra said. She'd been busy on the phone.

"No foster homes?"

Myra shook her head. "Filled to overflowing with a waiting list."

"No temporary shelter of any kind?"

"Juvenile Hall."

"I ain't goin' to Juvie. Jerome, don't let them send me to Juvie." Kenisha shot up off the couch and darted over to Jerome. He put his arm around her.

"I won't," he said. "She'd be safer here with me than she would be at Juvie. You know that Mz. Boutwell."

I jumped in. "OK, here's what we're going to do, if it's alright with Myra. I'll take her home with me. She can stay with me until a good place can be found. OK?"

Myra looked surprised. "Roberta, let's talk about this outside for just a minute. Excuse us, please?" She grabbed my sleeve and pulled me off the couch and out the door. It was 5 o'clock and dark already. The wind was picking up and I pulled my hood tighter around my head.

"What do you think you're doing, Roberta? You shouldn't be getting involved in this mess. And besides you're not certified as a foster." Myra's wool hat was pulled down to her eyebrows and made her look funny, but there was no humor in our discussion.

"Well, Jerome's not certified either, and I'm pretty darn sure Calvin's not. It's just for a night or two, and we know she'll be safe with me, at least."

"What about your son? What about Jack?"

"He's got a job, now, so he's gone all day, and Kenisha will be in school. I'll be there when she gets home. Besides, he's almost 50 and I'm pretty sure he'll ignore her completely. He may be a little shocked at his new 'sister', but I don't think he'll mind. He's too wrapped up in his own stuff to care."

"This is highly irregular, you know."

"Oh, come on, Myra. That sounds so, so...bureaucratic. Let's just do what's best for Kenisha here. Sending her to Juvie just isn't it. Unless, of course, you could take her home with you." A bit of a challenge, there.

"My in-laws are visiting just now so we are already bursting at the seams. Or I would." Myra sounded a mite defensive.

"What about that aunt who lives around here and is supposed to supervise these kids when their mom goes to rehab? Could you ask her?"

"I did a home visit on her. She's got umpty-ump kids living with her already. I doubt she could protect Kenisha from Calvin."

"OK, then. The best solution for right now is for me to take Kenisha home with me. Agreed?"

Myra nodded. She seemed reluctant, but she didn't argue any more. We went back in and told Kenisha and

Jerome. "I'm going to take you to my house for a day or two. After that we'll work something out."

Kenisha looked at Jerome. He nodded. "Go get your stuff," he said.

Kenisha disappeared down the hall and came back a few minutes later carrying a brown grocery bag stuffed with her belongings. She and Jerome whispered together and then he hugged her.

"Call me every day," he said.

"I will." Kenisha's lower lip quivered.

Myra put her arm around Kenisha's shoulders and gently moved her toward the door. "This is just for a few days, you know. We'll get it worked out so you can either come home, or go to some nice place until the baby comes. It will be OK. You'll see."

Jerome stopped me before I got to the door. "I don't know you or even where you live. You better be good to her."

"Jerome, she'll be safe with me and it won't be for very long." I pulled a pen and a slip of paper from my purse. "Here's my address. It's out in Kensington. Also, here's my phone number. Why don't you give me yours, too?"

As we exchanged information little frissons of doubt began to fire in my brain. Where would she sleep? How would she get to school? Whose bathroom would she share, mine or Jack's? What am I doing?

Out loud I said, "Honey, we all just want what's best for Kenisha. Being where Calvin might hurt her is dangerous. She's a great kid and deserves better. If I can do anything for her, I will... and you, too. Just let me know."

Going down the steps to join Myra and Kenisha I held on tight to the handrail.

Chapter 8

"Mother! Who is that?" Jack whispered, coming into the kitchen where I was putting things out for an impromptu supper. I'd missed him when he came in from work. I'd planned to warn him.

"That's Kenisha. She's going to spend a night or two with us."

"She's black."

"I know."

"And she's pregnant."

"I know."

"What's she doing here?"

I explained the situation. "It's just temporary, to keep her safe from a very mean brother. She needs our help, Jack. We will both be kind to her. Won't we? I said, won't we?"

Before he could reply Kenisha joined us. "This your son, Mz. Fischer? Hi, I'm Kenisha."

Taken by surprise Jack responded, "Hi, I'm Jack. Stay out of my room."

Un-phased, Kenisha shot back, "I'll stay out of your room if you stay out of mine. Deal?"

I chuckled to myself. Kenisha was no push-over and obviously had well-polished negotiating skills. Learned from an early age, I'd bet.

"Supper's almost ready. Will you eat with us, Jack?"

"No thanks. I'll get something later." He gave Kenisha a hard stare and went to his room. He came back all bundled up and headed out the back door. "See you later." He slammed the door behind him.

"I don't think he likes me."

"Jack's an only child and not used to sharing very much. Remember, he just got out of prison and he's suspicious of everyone. I think he'll get over it. We'll just be nice to him. You know, like the salesman at the Mall."

"What'd he do?"

"He tried to rob a bank."

"Oh."

"He had a problem with drugs and alcohol and I wouldn't give him the money he needed to support that. So, he tried to rob a bank. Of course he couldn't get drugs in prison and hopefully he'll stay clean now. He's supposed to go to AA meetings."

"One of my uncles was in prison for a while. He got drugs in there all the time."

I looked at her in disbelief. "Are you sure?"

"Oh, yes, ma'am. He laughed about it at our house when he got out."

A boot kicked my stomach. Was I not living in the real world?

"Yes, well, sit down there and we'll have supper. Jack will just have to eat our leftovers."

Kenisha was like a cat investigating the nooks and crannies of my home. I left her alone, but could hear her murmurs. "Wow. Look at all them books. That's a pretty chair. Nice. Oh, a washer and a dryer. Neat." And her questions.

"Mz. Fischer, is this your computer? Oh, is this your boy's room?" And moving on, "What bathroom can I use? Is it all right if I take a bath now?"

We fixed up a futon in my tiny third bedroom, and shifted my ironing board and other junk into different storage spaces. There was an old dresser that had been my mother's, a rickety rocker from a yard sale, and a child's desk left over from Jack's youth that made up the furnishings. I also added a telephone extension, as I knew keeping in touch with her family and Tasha would be important to her. Kenisha loved them all. By the second day she was calling it 'my room' and spending time there doing her homework and just 'chillin'. Her word, not mine. I could hear her on the phone talking to Jerome and Tasha, and once, even her mother.

Our ménage-a-trois lasted longer than I thought, almost a month. Nothing opened up in the foster home arena, and Juvenile Hall was a dismal last resort that no one wanted Kenisha to suffer. With the help of Myra, Social Services gave me a temporary foster certificate that would last a couple of months. That gave us breathing room. I understood that Social Services was working hard to find a good place for her. And of course her delivery date was coming closer all the time. In the meantime she was still in school and taking part in the Teen Moms programs.

My challenge was to expose Kenisha to the larger world. But it couldn't seem to be beyond the reach of a project girl. Where could I begin? I talked to all my friends and took a second, different look at my own activities. T'ai Chi? Probably not, in her very pregnant state. The Recorder Consort? Maybe. Pretty dull for a teenager, though. Newcomers Club? Hmm, no. What then?

One day I needed to go to the big new main library and asked Kenisha to ride along. She'd never been there, she said, although she was a regular at her school library. The minute we walked in the front doors I knew I had discovered the Comstock Lode for Kenisha. She stood there with her mouth hanging wide, her eyes staring, her head swiveling in all directions. I herded her to the information desk and turned her loose on the staff member there while I went off to take care of my own business. Call it serendipity or happy happenstance or whatever you will, the staff member was a young black woman who responded to Kenisha's eager questions with matching enthusiasm. I watched from a distance as she put a call bell at the front of her desk and started a tour for this youngster with a thirst she didn't yet know she had.

I was sitting on a comfortable sofa reading a magazine when they returned from their tour. Kenisha was clutching a small stack of books under her arm and a new library card in the other hand. Her face shone and her eyes sparkled.

I stood and introduced myself to Rosa Bland, by her name tag, the staff member. "Thanks for doing that. I think you may have a new regular customer here."

"Listen, any time. I'm thrilled to have Kenisha come in. You be sure and come back, now, you hear?" She smiled at Kenisha and returned to her desk.

"What books did you get?" I asked when we were back in the car.

"Well, there's one about famous women, like Maya Angelou, you know. And a couple about careers. The library lady helped me pick them out."

"Sound like good choices. What did you think of the library?"

She chattered the rest of the way home about all of its wonders. As we pulled into the driveway she commented, "Wouldn't it be fun to have a job like that library lady? I wish I could do that."

Very casually I noted, "You can, if you want to."

Another day we stopped by the Valley Pet Vets Clinic where Kate Miller was the office manager. We served on the SNIP board together and I needed to pick up some material for an up-coming board meeting. Kenisha came in with me. Kate met us and I asked if we could get the tour of the facilities. I didn't want Kenisha to see into the operating room where once I had watched as a mother cat was opened up and her unborn kittens in little sacs were removed. I needn't have worried, though, as it was late afternoon, and all the work for the day had been completed. The staff members were gathered in the break room laughing and chatting, but stopped to be introduced to me and Kenisha.

They were a mixed group with varied backgrounds. One of the veterinarians was a Korean man, the other a young redheaded woman. The vet techs were a lively bunch, black, white, tan, all united in giving the docs a hard time about something that had happened that day.

Kate and I went into her office to talk and Kenisha was given a tour of the clinic by one of the vet techs.

Back in the car Kenisha said, "I asked that lady, Jill, what a vet tech was and she told me it meant Veterinary Technician. She said you have to go to school for about 18 months to get to be one. I asked if it was hard and she said it was, but mostly you have to love animals, and not be too squeamish. What's that mean, Mz. Fischer? Squeamish?" After I explained she added, "I never thought about work being fun, before. They was sure having fun. And you could tell they all liked each other. That's nice."

I felt certain that picture in her mind was much more powerful than any lecture I could give on the subject. We rode home in silence, but the thoughts bouncing around inside the car were palpable.

Sometimes in the evenings we'd watch TV together or just visit. I steered the conversation to promote staying in school. Kenisha steered it to keeping her baby. I could hardly encourage putting her child up for adoption when a prime example of the results, at least in one case, was visible every day, right here, and not very pretty.

My days were full, sometimes too full. I took Kenisha to where her school bus picked her up in the mornings, then met her after school for the ride home. She could get to Teen Moms on her own, so on the days I worked she often met me there. Between those trips I kept up my T'ai Chi classes, my rehearsals with the recorder group, and my activities with the Newcomers' Club. Al-Anon two days a week was a must. Sometimes those were followed by lunches with Dan. I also had lunches with Myra where we discussed Kenisha, and coffee shop rendezvous with Julie where we discussed Jack......and Dan. If I had an hour or two to myself I'd settle in my recliner, put my feet up, and open a book. Later, when I woke up, my joints would ache and I'd groan getting out of the chair. I wasn't making much progress with the book.

Chapter 9

Jack was in the picture, too, but not much. He left to go to work before I got up and often came home too late for supper with me and Kenisha. Sometimes he ate before he came home, other times he raided the fridge. He talked very little but as far as I could tell he appeared to be OK. He spent most evenings out someplace. He didn't tell me where, and I didn't ask. He was a grown man, after all. During the week he was home by 10:30 or 11:00. On weekends he was sometimes gone all night. Again, I didn't ask.

I was cooking supper one evening when Jack came slamming in the back door. "That Pete is just stupid! He's a real jackass." He dragged off his cap, and tore off his coat. He threw them at a chair where they slid off and fell onto the floor.

"Why? What did he do? I thought you liked your boss." These scenes always puzzled me.

"He wants me to stack lumber." He stalked across the kitchen, opened the refrigerator and peered inside.

"What's wrong with that?"

He turned and gave me a dirty look. "Because I have a bad back, that's what wrong. I told you that. I told him that, too, but he didn't believe me. He's just a …" He trailed off as if he understood the expression on my face. I was sure an 'f' word had been imminent.

"Why can't we ever have any beer in here? I need a beer now and then, you know." He swung the door closed and scowled at me.

I didn't remember anything about a bad back. "What are you going to do? And pick those things up off the floor." I waved my cooking spoon at his coat and hat.

I tasted the stew and added some salt. My biggest challenge during these 'events' was to keep my cool.

"I'll talk to Robert tomorrow. He's Pete's boss. He better believe me 'cause I'm not going to stack lumber. I'll quit first." He picked up his clothing and stomped through the kitchen and on down the hall. "Is that girl still here?" he called back.

"Kenisha. She's visiting over in the Roosevelt Homes. Myra's with her."

"I'll eat supper here, then. After I take a shower."

I was pleased to think we'd have some time together to talk. Just mother and son together in civilized conversation again. It was overdue. Perhaps we could discuss his problems and I could help him find answers. No. Strike that. Just a nice conversation would be a big step forward.

He came in the kitchen with his hair slicked back and his skin pink from the hot water. He'd changed into a clean sweat shirt with a fierce looking wolf on the front and exchanged his work boots for the Adidas.

He plopped down at the table and without pause, or waiting for me to join him, helped himself to the stew. With his forearms on the table he bent his head and shoveled the food into his mouth. Prison manners had obviously overtaken those we'd worked so hard to instill in him as a child.

I'd made a jello salad and put a piece on small plates with a lettuce leaf underneath and a dab of mayonnaise on top. He scraped the mayo off and devoured the jello in two bites, leaving the lettuce leaf behind.

"This must taste good to you. Stew was one of your favorites, and you always loved carrot and pineapple salad."

"Maybe I'll just quit." No small talk here, obviously.

"But you just got the job." My protest sounded weak.

"I ain't taking shit off of no one." He shoved back his chair and stood. "That's a stupid place to work. They're all assholes down there."

With that he left the table, and in a few minutes banged out the door. Not even a goodbye. What had happened? He had loved his job and all the people in the store. Why the sudden change? I was mystified. So much for another of my pipe dreams. I finished my stew, put my untouched jello back in the fridge, and got out the Rocky Road.

Myra and Kenisha arrived soon after Jack left. I could hear them arguing before they got in the house and I shoved the ice cream back in the freezer. Kenisha burst in first. "I wanna go home. Don't nobody there want me to give up my baby. And I miss Jerome and Tasha, and my mama. I even miss stupid old Calvin." Her lower lip was quivering.

Myra followed her in. Looking at me, she rolled her eyes, and made a face.

"I'm sure you do," I said. "It's hard to be away from home. Why don't you go get out of your things and we'll talk about it. I've got some jello salad here you might like." It takes a real emergency to make me share my Rocky Road.

"What happened?" I asked Myra as soon as Kenisha went down the hall.

"Nothing, really. Tasha and Jerome were there, and so was her mother. They were all happy to see her and gave her big hugs and everything. I think her mother may even have been sober. No sign of Calvin, though."

Kenisha came back and sat down to eat the jello. "This is good. Is there any more?"

While I dished out more jello I said, "I have some stew I could warm up in a minute if you'd like some of that." Kenisha nodded.

"Myra, don't you want some, too?"

"I've got to get home to my family, thanks."

I popped some stew in the microwave and said to Kenisha, "Sounds like you had a nice visit. Did you get to see everyone you wanted to?"

"Mama was there, and Jerome and Tasha. They want me to come home. And I really want to go, Mz. Fischer. It's been nice here and all, but they my family. I need to be with my family."

While Kenisha had her head down eating the stew I raised an eyebrow at Myra.

She nodded. "She probably needs to go back. I'd rather she didn't, but it'll be OK, I think."

"What about Calvin?"

Kenisha looked up. "Calvin promised Mama he'd leave me alone."

I contemplated while moving dishes around aimlessly. If I pushed for having her stay, I knew it would be more for me than for her. I really did like having her around. As for making a dent in her decision to keep her baby, I'd made no progress at all.

"Tell you what. It's too late to take you home tonight, so I'll take you tomorrow after school. How would that be?"

"Really? To stay?" Her happy face would break anyone's heart.

"If that's what you want. We're not taking prisoners here, just trying to keep you safe and happy."

When Myra was gone and Kenisha tucked in, I finished up the Rocky Road.

I felt sad. I knew I'd miss her a lot.

Chapter 10

We went to dinner first, then the play. It was the musical 'Oliver' and the cast of teenaged singers and actors was amazing. We joined in the standing ovation and applauded until our hands stung. Afterwards we stopped in at a place called 'Barnies' for a night cap.

We picked a cushioned wicker love seat against one wall and settled in comfortably. Dan asked the waiter for some Drambuie. I wanted a Bailey's Irish Cream over slivered ice. A little group was playing Rogers and Hammerstein numbers quietly in a far corner. Live plants in colorful pots were scattered through the room giving it a homey feel. A couple at the bar had their heads together, laughing softly. Our drinks came and were placed on a low table in front of us.

An entertaining guy, Dan talked about his life. I talked about mine. It was obvious we had little in common aside from our sons. His mother and father were teachers. My dad drove a truck. He'd always lived in Midsouth City. I'd moved more than 20 times, sometimes with my soldier husband, sometimes on my own. We did share over-developed senses of humor. We laughed a lot, having more fun than anyone else in the place. It occurred to me that this was the first time I'd been in a bar with a man late at night for a very long time. I was feeling quite cosmopolitan. I even wished I still smoked so I could casually tap the ash off and peer mysteriously through the smoke. I loved it. Finally, reluctantly, we agreed it was time to leave. Dan paid our tab. I made a quick trip to the ladies'.

The night was crystal clear with a bright moon. But cold. Very cold. I took Dan's arm as we walked to his car. It felt nice to have a man to hang on to. At home he walked me to my door and I thanked him for the nice evening.

"I had a nice time, too. It was fun. Let's have a hug."

Hugs are good. I often hug my women friends. Hugging Dan felt better. My cheek rubbed against his whiskers and my lips brushed his ear. Oops.

I closed the door behind me and just stood there. Grinning. It was dark in the house. I turned on lights and peeked into the bedrooms. Kenisha's was empty, of course. Jack's was, too. I'd spent many years comfortably alone in my own home but tonight it felt empty. I double checked the doors and went to bed. As I lay there waiting for sleep to come I started to laugh. Out loud. "Bertie girl, you've got a boyfriend. Is that a hoot, or what?"

There was no black dog dream that night.

Jack didn't quit his job, nor get fired apparently. He came and went to work as before, but he had stopped talking to me. I tried to watch for signs of drugs or alcohol, but didn't see anything suspicious. But then, how would I know?

He came in late one evening and I asked, "Where've you been?" I didn't mean it to be confrontational.

"Same place I always go. To the bowling alley over there on Whitaker. What do you care?"

"Jack, I was just curious as to how you spend your time. I didn't know you bowled."

"There's a bar there, Mother. I just hang out at the bar. Is that all right?"

"Oh, Jack, please. I'm your mother, not your jailor. I'm not trying to pick a fight, just have a conversation. We don't talk anymore."

"Not much to talk about. You're all tied up with that Kenisha girl, and that guy Dan. You don't have any time for me."

"We have some time now. Kenisha's back at home and Dan's not here. My time is your time. Besides, they're just people I know, not people I love, like you. You're my son."

"Yeah, right."

"What in the world is the matter with you, Jack? You're living here, you eat my food, I do your laundry. I don't ask too many questions about where you go and what you do. I haven't pressed you for the $100 you owe me. I'm here to talk to you if you want me to. What is it you want?" My voice and my blood pressure were rising.

"You wouldn't understand." He headed back toward his room.

To his back I shouted, "I can't understand if you won't tell me."

He slammed his bedroom door. How could I understand if he wouldn't tell me?

That night the black dog returned. I could hear him barking and barking.

I woke up in a sweat and the barking stopped.

***

Early one Saturday Julie called and told me to stay home instead of meeting her at CuppaJava as usual. She was coming over, she said. I thought it strange, but put on the pot and thawed out some sticky buns I'd been saving for a rainy day. Jack was sleeping in. The phone woke him when Julie called and he got up, went to the bathroom then back to bed.

I heard Julie drive up. It took her a long time before she banged on the storm door. I opened the inside door. She stood there in her red tennis shoes, stylish jeans, and torn YALE sweat shirt holding a box covered with a towel.

"Open the door, my hands are full."

"I see. What's that?" My reluctant heart thought it knew.

"You'll see. Open the door." She was grinning from ear to ear as she came up the steps. "You're going to love this."

"Wanna bet?" I followed her into the kitchen where she placed the box on the floor and flipped the towel away.

"Ta da!" She acted like a proud momma.

Sure enough. I could see two kitties peering up at me somberly. Julie picked one up and handed it to me. It was white with large tan and black patches on its back and sides. Its pink little nose sniffed delicately. She picked up the other one and held it against her chest. It was a tiger. Striped orange with a little white mixed in.

"We've been calling this one T. J. and that one Patches. You can name them anything you want."

"Oh, Julie. I can't keep animals. I'm too old, and I'm gone a lot and…and… they'll get lonely."

"That's why I brought you two. They keep each other company."

"I don't even have a litter box."

"I know. I brought you one. Here, hold T. J. while I go get it."

What I was trying to do was say 'No'. But the kittens were pushing their little moist noses up against mine and rubbing their furry faces across my cheeks. Julie brought in a litter box and shoved it under the kitchen table.

"Oh, that's a nice place for it." I said. I put the kittens on the floor and they scrambled under the table and tumbled into the litter box. They used it very efficiently, scratched at the litter, then hopped out and started nosing about the kitchen.

"Well, at least they're house broken. Oh, OK. But just as a foster, you know. Just until you can adopt them out."

"Oh, sure," Julie said brightly. I knew she was lying.

I found an old cereal bowl and started to pour some milk in it. "This is skim. I suppose they should have regular, huh?"

"Actually, milk's not good for cats, Roberta. You should give them water instead. I brought some canned cat food to get you started. They like the dry stuff, too."

"But you always see pictures of cats lapping up milk, and we always gave our cats milk when I was a little girl."

"Many cats are lactose intolerant it turns out. And besides, can you think of any other animal that drinks milk except from its own mother?" Julie was obviously 'up' on animal care.

Oh, honestly. I dumped out the milk and replaced it with water from the tap.

We sat at the table drinking decaf coffee with sugar free hazelnut flavored creamer and eating sticky, pecan topped cinnamon buns. I opened the Saturday section of my day-of-the week pill holder, and swallowed the contents, making sure the one for high-sugar was included. Can't be too careful, at my age.

We watched the cats playing together on the floor. They were cute, you had to give them that.

"What's going on?" Jack said, padding barefoot into the kitchen.

"Look what Julie brought us," I said, nodding toward the kittens. "Did you meet Julie before you, uh, went away?"

"I don't think so. Hey," he grunted in her general direction. He knelt down and reached out for the kittens. "Hi, little fellas. Come here to me. Are you going to keep them, Mom?"

"I guess so." That was a commitment I really didn't want to make.

"Hi, Jack," said Julie. "We have a big load of kitties right now and ran out of foster homes for them all. I thought you and your mom might enjoy having these two around."

"Cool. This one's mine." He was holding T. J. "What's his name?"

"We've been calling him T. J. but you can call him anything you want."

Jack thought a minute. "I'll call him Tigger, I think. Hey, Tigger. Want to go see my room?" Jack rubbed the kitten's nose with his own and wandered off down the hall. Patches followed on Jack's heels, meowing loudly. "OK, OK, you can come, too. Come on."

"Well, what do you know? I'd forgotten how much he loved animals when he was a kid." My voice quivered a bit.

Julie reached over and patted my hand. "Maybe this is just what he needs. Animal therapy has proven to be very effective in some situations." Julie could sound awfully clinical at times.

I got up and closed the doors to the rest of the house. "I'm just so frustrated, Julie. He won't talk to me. And one day he thinks the guys at work are just great then he calls them all assholes. He hangs out at a bar almost every evening, and I don't know where he spends his Saturday nights. I thought he couldn't get drugs in prison but Kenisha said her uncle got them all the time when he was in jail. Jack's supposed to be going to AA or NA, but I don't know whether he does or not. I suppose his parole officer will be checking on that. This just seems like a huge nightmare that never goes away. I'm so tired of it."

"I know you must be." Julie leaned over and patted my hand. "But, you know, I think Jack's behavior is not just 'bad boy' stuff. I think he may have a…well…a mental disorder of some kind. And if that's the case, then he needs more help than you can give him. I wish you'd look into that, Berta. At least give it some thought."

Julie's insistence that Jack might have a mental disorder really wounded me, but I tried not to let her see my hurt. I'd read somewhere that if a child had a mental disability of any kind, it was the mother's fault. I had tried as hard as I could to be a good mother. I remember losing my temper a number of times, but not any more than most mothers I was sure. Besides, seeing Jack with the kittens gave me hope that he would begin to feel more normal after all those years in prison. It must be hard to make the transition from incarceration to freedom, and he probably just needed a little more time.

Chapter 11

The winter was starting to ease. I saw my first robin, a good sign. The snow was suddenly gone and some trees were starting to show tiny buds. A brave crocus poked its purple head up in my front yard. March had come in like a lamb, but was blustering its way through the rest of the month. Some of the neighbors were starting to venture out and one day Jenna Barr from across the street, and Phyllis Newberry my next door neighbor on the other side from Howard, were standing out on the sidewalk visiting. I sauntered over to join them, although as I drew nearer I sensed that I'd been the subject of their conversation.

"Hi, Jenna, Phyllis. Feels good to be able to get out of the house, doesn't it? Seemed like a long winter. How are you two doing?"

Phyllis pulled a face that looked as if she'd caught a whiff of something smelly. "Bill and I are fine, Roberta. And how are you? Seems you've had some, uh, unusual guests at your house recently."

Ah, the source of the dreadful smell unveiled. I glanced at Jenna and saw her frowning and trying to distance herself from Phyllis' remark. I can never resist pulling someone's leg if they stick it out right in front of me. "Oh, really? And who would that be?" As if I didn't know.

"Well, that, that, uh that Negro girl who looks awfully pregnant, for one." Phyllis is probably in her 60's and I think moved here from some place in Mississippi. She waddles around their yard in a tattered house coat with curlers in her hair directing her nice husband as he works in the garden.

"Actually, I think we call them African American these days, Phyl. Her name is Kenisha and she has an IQ of 150. I wish mine were that high. Frankly, I'm proud to have her as a guest in my home." With a look of distaste on my face I turned away and went back toward my house.

Jenna scuttled along behind me. "I'm sorry, Berta. I just want you to know I don't feel that way. I'm glad you set her straight."

I sighed. "Thanks, Jenna. Unfortunately some folks can't seem to get beyond the race thing, but I keep hoping." Jenna drifted back across the street and went in her house.

I glimpsed Howard out walking around his house, looking for winter damage it seemed. We would soon need to replace our feeders with bird houses for nesting. Then our competition changed to 'who got the best birds' in their boxes. Blue birds would take top honors, and all but sparrows were welcome.

When Kenisha first left my house and went home she called me quite often, but later, not so much. So when I was at Teen Moms on a Monday near the end of the month I knew she was due to see Myra and I was anxious to see her.

I plunked on the computer and kept one eye on the door. Then she was there. I watched her come slowly and carefully through the door. Her time was quickly approaching I thought. I was disturbed at the way she looked. Not very clean, and although her belly was huge, her face was thin and worn looking. She smiled at me rather wanly I thought, shuffled over to my desk and lowered herself into my side chair.

"Hey, Mz. Fischer."

"Hey, Kenisha. I'm so happy to see you. How are you doing?"

"Oh, OK I guess. But this is hard. Lots harder than I thought it was going to be."

Oh, honey, wait 'til the baby cries all night and you are never able to get any sleep. And you can't go anyplace without taking it along or leaving it with someone you might not trust, and…. Then tell me how hard it is. But I didn't say that.

"I'm sure it is, honey. How much longer, do you know?"

"Not really. The doctor says she could come early, but he don't know for sure."

"How are things at home?"

"Momma's finally in rehab and you know they took the little kids away. I haven't seen them for a long time. Calvin's being, well, pretty good, and Jerome is at home as much as he can be. My auntie across the way makes sure everything is OK."

That information caught me off guard. I thought they were going to find a better situation for her. It seemed no one had done a thing. I couldn't wait to talk to Myra.

"How's school?"

"It's too hard, Mz Fischer. I don't feel good most of the time. I stopped going a couple of weeks ago."

"Oh, Kenisha. I'm so sorry. How are you spending your time?"

Instead of answering she changed the subject. "How's it at your house? Is my room still there? How's Jack doing?"

"Oh, we're doing OK, and yes, your room is still there. Maybe you could come visit us one day. We have some kittens now."

"That would be nice. But I gotta go see Mz. Boutwell, now." She hoisted herself up out of the chair. "Bye."

I hated that my brain didn't crank out ideas as quickly as it did when I was 35. Belatedly it came to me that Kenisha had offered me a clue when she asked if her room was still there. Maybe she was angling for an invitation to return to my house.

When she came back to the reception area I called her over. A question had been bothering me, so I asked it. "Do you know how you're going to get to the hospital when the time comes?"

"Same way I go to the doctor, I s'pose. Call a cab."

Now I was really angry. This was a baby having a baby, not a grown woman giving birth. Just call a cab? Yeah, right!

"Listen, why don't you come visit me for a few days? You can play with the kittens and we can eat ice cream and watch old movies. I have a whole bunch of new ones on tape, and we could go to the library and get some you'd like." We grinned at each other, having discovered that our movie tastes were quite different.

"Really. I could come get you tomorrow. You could tell your Aunt and Jerome what you're going to do, and get some of your things together to stay for a few days. I'm serious. It'll be fun."

And I can get you cleaned up and your clothes washed and some good healthy food in you. And should you have to go to the hospital I'll take you there myself and stay with you while the baby comes. My mind raced.

A smile lit her face. "Really, Mz. Fischer? But I have to ask my auntie and Jerome."

"Of course. Have your aunt call me if she wants to. And you call me and let me know if they say it's OK."

As soon as she went out the door I stormed to Myra's office.

"I can't believe this child, this...this baby, is expected to just call a cab when she goes into labor. And what happened to finding her a decent place to live when she comes home from the hospital?" I was shouting.

Myra looked stunned. "Here, sit down, Roberta. Let me get you a cup of coffee."

"I don't want a cup of coffee. I want to know why Kenisha is expected to manage all this by herself. She's a child, for heaven's sake. Don't you people get it?"

"Let's go in the conference room," Myra said. My shouting had the other caseworkers poking their heads above the partitions of the cubbies they called their offices.

The conference room had walls all the way to the ceiling. Chairs surrounded the one long table. Myra closed the door after us and pulled out a chair, indicating one across the table for me to use. I was too mad to sit down.

"Please, Roberta, sit down. There are some things you need to hear."

Reluctantly I eased my old bones onto the metal folding chair. My blood was still boiling.

"Do you know how many girls from the projects are currently in the Teen Moms program?"

"Of course I do. I keep the statistics on the computer. Right now you have 135."

"And do you think Kenisha's situation is any different from the other 134 girls?"

"I don't know, and I don't care. Do they all have brothers like Calvin who'll beat them up given half a chance? And a mother who's a junkie in rehab, and no father to speak of?"

"I don't know about the brothers, but all of the girls have mothers who are single and on welfare. A good many of them probably are junkies. And no one has a real father. It's not a pretty picture, Roberta. And Kenisha is just one small part of it. I wish it were different, but it isn't. All we can do here at Teen Moms is give them some education in parenting, hook them into the services that will be available to them and their babies, and try to show them that there is a better world out there if they are willing to work hard enough to get themselves there." Myra was beginning to steam up a bit herself.

"OK, then what about Social Services? What are they doing? I thought they were trying to find Kenisha a better place to live. What about that?"

"They do the best they can, but there are few if any 'better' places for these teens after their baby comes. The best we can hope for is that their own home is ready to take on a new baby. It won't be a first for most of their homes, you know."

"So they were really lying to us when they told us they would find a better place for her, and we were lying to her when we told her the same thing. Myra, I don't like to be lied to, and I don't like to lie. This is pathetic." I was shouting again.

Myra leaned forward and put her hands flat on the table. "Would you just calm down, please? You're missing part of the puzzle here. What you probably haven't experienced in the projects is their sense of *community*. It's mostly women and children and they have a fierce pride in looking after each other. Yes, they're poor. Yes, drug use is rampant. Yes, the children get pregnant and have children. But when there's trouble they come together like, like ants on spilled sugar. When the babies are born they have a whole network of women who pitch in and see that things are taken care of. They all know the government 'systems' and work them like pro's. Many are grandmas who have been dangling a baby off their hip since they were teens. There's not much they don't know about taking care of a baby. And most of all? These women love those babies. So, yes, we 'get' it, Roberta. Just make sure you do."

Well! I felt chastened. I sat back in my chair and looked sheepishly at Myra. I remembered my own advice to new non-profit executives. "Don't go in there acting like everything they ever did was stupid and now you're Captain Kleen here to make everything right." Suddenly I felt pretty stupid. That's exactly what I'd been doing.

"OK. I see what you're saying. I suppose I did jump to conclusions."

It took a while for my blood pressure to come down and I continued to feel a bit belligerent. I could not leave without a parting shot. "Well, the least they can do is neuter the guys making these little girls pregnant. A snip here, a snip there…. If we can do it to animals, why not do it to those perverts?"

"I'd certainly vote for that, Roberta."

"I owe you an apology, Myra. Sorry."

"What you're doing for Kenisha? It's good. I wish we had more Roberta's who would take an interest in these girls. Just remember that in the end, they do have to go home again."

I went back to my desk, got my purse, and left.

Roosevelt Homes looked different through my newly opened eyes. The coming of Spring helped, too. The gray/white desolation of winter was replaced by green sprouts of grass in the open areas between buildings. A troop of Girl Scouts was making a sweep through the project, wearing heavy gloves and picking up trash and putting it in bags, living out their "do a good deed daily" motto. I knew the members were all project girls because Kenisha had told me about them. One young man had been conscripted to dig up a small plot for a garden and was being closely supervised by two crones, hands on hips, standing over him. Small groups of women and little children sat on 'stoops' in the pale sunshine, talking and laughing. They looked at me and nodded as I passed, their veiled, suspicious eyes following to see where I was going. I had to weave my way through gangs of boisterous children racing up and down the sidewalks and stairways.

Kenisha sat on a chair outside her door, a sack of her belongings by her side. She introduced me to the woman with her. "This is my auntie, Mz. Fischer. She wants to meet you."

"Auntie" was a small woman with surprising green eyes. A short Afro framed a pleasant round face and she wore glasses that gave her a scholarly look. She inspected me closely and said, "Mz. Fischer. I'm Gloria Swanson." She laughed and added, "No, ma'am, not that one. Not that movie star Gloria Swanson."

She had a baby on her hip, and a toddler clinging to the hem of her cotton print dress. "Wanta thank you for being nice to Kenisha. Mighty kind of you. Mighty kind."

"I'm glad to meet you, too, Ms. Swanson. Kenisha's sort of special, I think." I smiled down at Kenisha, sitting there looking terribly pregnant, and very young.

"Yes'um. We think so, too. She say you're worried about her getting to the hospital?"

"Well, yeah. I'd sort of wondered."

"Don't you worry none. We'll see she gets there in fine shape. Lots of folks around here helping me keep an eye on her and Jerome. Calvin, too. She's doing OK."

She sounded a bit defensive so I said, "I hope it's alright with you if I take her out to my house for a few days, sort of like a vacation? We have some new kittens she can play with and maybe I can help her with her homework." To Kenisha I said, "And there's ice cream in the freezer."

"Be nice if she could finish this semester at school. That'd be mighty good of you. Yes, ma'am. Mighty good." She switched the baby to the other hip and took the toddler by the hand. "Bye, sweetie, you be good

now. Call me, hear? Nice to meet you, Mz. Fischer."
Gloria Swanson walked away.

"You ready?"

Kenisha struggled to her feet and picked up her bag
of belongings. "Yes, ma'am. What kind of ice cream?"

As we walked back along the sidewalks to my car, the
onlookers watched, and commented. "Bye, Kenisha."
"See you later, girl." "Don't get lost, now, hear?" They
wanted me to know that she belonged to them, and I
wasn't to forget it. I got the picture.

The kittens and Kenisha were soon fast friends. They
climbed on the bed with her, and followed her around the
house. She talked to them, telling secrets I doubt she
shared with anyone. When Jack came home from work
that first day I wondered how he'd react to this competition for their affection. To my surprise they joined in a
foursome to play together on the floor in her room. Jack
and Kenisha talked to Tigger and Patches and soon they
were talking to each other. At first it was just cat talk,
but later on I overheard some q. and a. about babies and
working and adoption. How I wished I could be a fly on
the wall, but I knew that if I intervened it would stop.

I put my usual activities on hold in order to spend
time with Kenisha. She spent hours in the bathroom, like
any teenager. We called in Myra to help with her hair,
cornrows not being in my parenting handbook. Her visits

replaced Kenisha's trips to Teen Moms, so their meetings were transferred to my living room. Sometimes I'd join them, if invited, and we'd talk about what was ahead for the teenage mommy-to-be. Putting the baby up for adoption seemed totally out of the question, although I still thought it a good idea. Myra was looking into a program at one of the local high schools where child care was available during class time for the young parents. Kenisha seemed enthusiastic about that. Transportation was a problem and would have to be worked out.

We drove to school and picked up her books and homework assignments. Her teachers greeted her warmly, and even the principal hugged her and wished her good luck. They urged me to call them if I had questions about the work. I had a college degree and didn't think I'd need to do that. I soon found out that the world had moved on since my school days, and I had much to learn. Kenisha and I would just have to learn it together.

Jerome and Tasha came to visit. They crowded into Kenisha's room with the kittens and closed the door. There was much laughter and loud music. Tasha's time was coming, too. The girls kicked Jerome out and closed the door, presumably to talk about things he didn't need to hear. He came to me in the kitchen and we talked about some things the girls didn't need to hear.

We started out talking about basketball, but soon moved on.

"What's Calvin doing these days?"

"Oh, he's still around. But he doesn't spend much time at home."

"I worry about him. Do you think he could hurt Kenisha or the baby?"

"Calvin's living in his own world. It doesn't include us, unless we get in his way. Then I don't know." His face showed the same concern that I was feeling.

He changed the subject. "I'm fixing up a room for Kenisha and the baby. I borrowed a crib and one of those little seats you carry babies in. The ladies bring stuff. They'll help her."

"Is there something you know of that Kenisha or the baby will need? Diapers? Blankets? Anything?"

"No, ma'am. I'll ask Auntie and the ladies. They'll know."

"OK, then. I'd like her to stay here with me until she goes into labor. I'll call you and you can meet us at the hospital. And let anyone, like your Aunt, know what's happening. Does that sound OK to you? I haven't asked her yet, but if you think it's a good idea I think she'll agree."

"Yes-um. That sounds fine. She likes it here and I can tell you're taking good care of her. And I'll have everything ready for when she brings the baby back to our house."

"Can Tasha come over again?" Kenisha asked a few days later. "She'll meet us at Teen Moms and come over here, if you don't mind taking her back to Roosevelt afterwards." Kenisha missed her best friend and she needed someone besides the kittens and Jack she could talk to like I talk to Julie.

"Sure, that's fine. If you tell me what you'd like for supper I'll get the stuff and you girls can fix it. How would that be?"

She was already on the phone to Tasha, discussing a menu. I wondered how I'd like tacos, 'skins, and coke. I put milk on my grocery list as well as fresh fruit.

The kitchen was a wreck when they finished, but the tacos were good and with fresh lettuce and tomatoes I figured they could pass the nutrition test. We put fresh sliced strawberries on top of our ice cream for dessert. I volunteered to clean up since they'd cooked, and they went off to Kenisha's room with the kittens.

About the time I finished wiping grease off the stove top and putting the last dishes away, I heard their voices raised in argument.

It sounded like that old song, "Yes, I can." "No, you can't." They came stomping into the kitchen, Tasha all dressed to go out.

"What's the problem?" I asked.

"We's having a difference of opinion." Tasha said, her nose in the air. "Can you take me home, now? Please ma'am?" She was an attractive girl, tall, very pregnant and with dark brown eyes sparking with anger.

I looked at Kenisha. She pursed her lips and turned her face away. No help there.

"Sure. Will you ride along, Kenisha?"

"No, thanks. I have homework to do." She turned and disappeared down the hall.

"Care to tell me what's going on?" I asked Tasha in the car.

"No, ma'am. I'd rather not discuss it." She turned and looked out the window.

I changed the subject. "Have you picked a name for your baby yet?"

"Yes, ma'am. I'm going to call him Michael. Michael Devon Turner."

"That's a nice name. Very dignified. Maybe he'll grow up to be a judge, or something like that."

Tasha was silent for a while then said, "Kenisha says she's going to finish high school and go to college. I told her that meant she'd have to give up her baby. That's what we were arguing about."

"I'm pretty sure she doesn't mean to give up the baby. We're trying to find ways for her to do both. It'll be hard, but I think it can be done. Do you think it's impossible to do both?"

"Just look at that Tamika lady. She give up her baby. I don't know no one that's kept their baby and finished school. Some have started but it's too hard and they drop out. And end up right back in Roosevelt anyhow."

"Well, I don't know the answer, but that's just not right. Anyone who wants to finish school and get out of the projects ought to be able to, don't you think?"

"Yes ma'am. But Kenisha's got someone like you to help her. Most of us don't have that."

We were quiet until I pulled to the curb in front of Tasha's apartment. "I hope you two will make up, Tasha. I think you need each other."

"I'm real mad at Kenisha, Mz. Fischer. If she calls and apologizes for being so uppity, then I'll think about it." She opened the door and started to step out.

"I'll talk to her, but remember you're her best friend and she loves you a lot. I'll watch till you get to your door, now. Good night."

Chapter 12

My love life was on hold. Dan kept asking me to accompany him to musical events or art shows around the city but I couldn't leave Kenisha. Once he even suggested we travel together on one of those bus tours to the Smokey Mountains, or somewhere. I told him I'd love to, but now was not a good time. I felt him slipping away and I didn't want that to happen.

Taking the bull by the horns following an Al-Anon meeting, I said to him, "How about coming to my house for supper one night?" I refused to consider the effects a pregnant teen-ager, two rambunctious kittens, and an often angry son might have on the evening. Surely God would take care of those details.

He accepted with alacrity and we settled on Friday evening at 7:00. I recruited Kenisha to help set the dining room table and make appetizers; crackers with a cream cheese spread topped with a piece of pimento. She thought them quite fancy. I worked readying the menu of grilled salmon, fresh asparagus, and couscous. They would cook quickly after Dan and I shared some wine and appetizers. Kenisha would take her appetizers to her room and join us for dinner. Salads were ready and in the fridge. Coffee ice cream and fancy, store-bought cookies would finish off the meal. The kittens slept, closed in Jack's room. There was no sign of Jack. I opened the wine and tested it. But where was Dan? At 7:15 he finally called to say he was on his way --- just leaving the house. That put his arrival time at about 7:35. Kenisha and I shared some of the appetizers. I drank a little more wine.

At 7:30 Jack banged in the back door and went straight to the fridge. "I'm starving. Is there anything to eat in this dump?"

I sighed. "Here, finish up these appetizers. I'll fix supper. Kenisha, set another place at the table, will you?"

Jack went back to his room, freeing the kittens that raced down the hallway to the kitchen, meowing loudly for their supper.

"Jack, come feed the kitties, will you?"

"When I get out of the shower." The bathroom door slammed.

"Kenisha?" The cats were rubbing around my ankles, and clawing up my legs, no doubt smelling the salmon I held on the broiler pan above my head.

"Yes, ma'am. I'll open a can." She was giggling.

I put the salmon under the broiler. The front door bell rang. "I'll go," I said.

Dan had dressed for the occasion in slacks, open collared shirt, and a tweed sport coat. He held a small bouquet of flowers, of the grocery store variety, and presented them to me solemnly. "Good evening, madam. Pretties for the pretty."

"Goodness, thank you. Come on in. We're in the kitchen."

Kenisha had the can open and was dishing cat food into a bowl. The one I'd planned to serve the asparagus in.

"Dan, this is Kenisha. Kenisha, this is my friend Dan. Dan, why don't you sit at the kitchen table while we finish up here?" I pointed him to a chair in the corner, farthest away from the vortex of Kenisha, cats, and the cook.

"H'lo," said Kenisha. "I made some appetizers, but we ate them already." In my head I added 'discuss social graces' to her homework list.

"I'm sorry I was late. I just dozed off, and woke up when my phone rang. Don't worry about the appetizers, Kenisha, but I'll bet they were good." He smiled at her. Handsome devil. Adorable beard.

I was standing there with the flowers in my hand taking a mental vote on whether to hunt up a vase, or get the couscous and asparagus going. Or pour Dan a glass of wine. Jack arrived, fresh out of the shower, bare-footed and bare-chested with tattoos in full bloom.

"Jack, could you pour Dan a glass of wine, please? Dan, this is my son Jack."

Dan stood up to shake hands and said, "Glad to meet you, Jack."

Jack put his hand out, gave a limp shake, and said, "Hey."

As he passed me to get the wine bottle, I hissed in his ear, "Then go put on some clothes."

I made a decision. I took the time to find a vase, fill it with water, and stick the flowers in. I put it on the table in front of Dan and suggested he rearrange them a bit. Then I turned to finishing the meal.

Jack returned, dressed to go out. "I'll just have a piece of the salmon, OK?" He pulled a portion out of the oven and put it on a piece of bread. "See you later." Out he went, eating his handheld supper.

On her own initiative Kenisha removed a place setting from the table. Then she went back and removed another. "I think I'll eat in my room, if that's OK, with you, Mz. Fischer." The little devil had the nerve to wink at me. I crossed off 'discuss social graces' from that homework list.

"That's fine, honey. I'll fix you a plate." The kittens had settled on Dan's lap. "Why don't you show Dan where Jack's room is so he can put Tigger and Patches in there?""

When Dan came back he reported that Kenisha wanted the kittens in with her. "I'm not sure who's going to get that salmon. I'm going to bet on the cats, though."

Our salmon was dried out from over cooking, the asparagus was nearly raw, but the couscous was perfect. We split the third salad, and made a big dent in the ice cream and cookies.

Dan proved to be more of a talker than a conversationalist. I was a good listener so the combination made for a comfortable evening. I spent the time looking at his hazel eyes with the long lashes and noticing what strong white teeth he had. His hands looked ineffectual, though, for someone who played the piano and organ. I remembered my mother saying she always noticed a man's hands.

He talked about his father who had taught at the local college but died when Dan was only eight years old. He talked about his mother and how she had raised him and his brother all on her own. He was launching into a discussion of his Aunt Ruth when I must have yawned because he suddenly jumped up.

"Oh, I'm sorry. I do go on. You've had a full day, I can tell," Dan said. "Why don't you go sit down in the living room and let me load your dishwasher. I'll make some coffee. It won't take a minute and then I'll join you."

Of course I demurred, but allowed him to prevail. What a nice guy.

I woke up when Jack shook my shoulder and said, "Mom, what are you doing out here? It's after midnight." I creaked up from the couch and looked around. Dan was gone. In the kitchen he had loaded the dishwasher, but pots and pans filled the sink. I poured out the pot of cold coffee. Down the hall Kenisha slept soundly in her bed with the kittens snuggled around her. Jack went into his room and closed the door. I slunk off to my bed thinking that this romance thing just might be too much for a person of a particular age. My age.

I had slept hard on the couch and then, comfortable in my bed, I couldn't go to sleep. My mind dwelt on Dan for a few minutes but with a good deal less enthusiasm than I'd felt before.

I then moved on to thinking about Jack. In junior high he was suspended for lighting a fire in someone's locker. The vice-principal told us he had a full file box on Jack's misdeeds. The other bad kids only had a file card or two. He finished Junior High because we sent him off to military school, but he never finished high school and was arrested and jailed more times over the years than I could count. Try as I might, I could not see beyond the dark curtain of his future.

I fell asleep feeling depressed. The black dog of my dreams showed up again and growled all night, rattling its chain. In the morning I was exhausted and felt as gray as the day. A cold rain rattling at the windows didn't help.

***

In the morning I got up, showered and then settled at the kitchen table with a bowl of cereal. Jack was making toast and fixing himself a cup of coffee.

"So, did you get paid yesterday?"

"Yeah. Wasn't much. They take most of it out for taxes and stuff."

"I want my $100 you know."

"I don't have $100. I had to pay back some guys at work that I borrowed from." Jack sat down across the table from me.

"Then pay me, say $25 a payday until you get me paid back. Remember, you didn't borrow from me, you robbed me. Besides, what are you borrowing money for? You're eating and sleeping here. I've been giving you money for the things you've said you need. Where's your money going?" My voice was starting to move up the scale.

"I bought a watch." He turned his wrist so I could see. It looked expensive. "And I'm getting new contacts. I need 'em, Mom. I really do." He was beginning to look fearful. As well he might.

I hated to get angry. But for me it wasn't a choice, the anger just welled up and exploded. When I opened my mouth the most awful garbage emerged. It was like nothing I'd ever heard, certainly from myself. It went on and on. I couldn't stop. Curse words. Nothing else.

Jack watched me, his eyes huge and his face dead white. Then he shoved his chair back from the table, picked up his coffee cup, and hurled it into the sink. The cup shattered and sprayed slivers across the counter and onto the floor. Without a word he slammed out of the house and walked away. Into the rain.

I leaned forward, my head on the heels of my hands, my eyes closed. Who was that fiend who blasted from my mouth unbidden? Who needed a therapist here? Me? Or Jack?

"Mz. Fischer? Are you OK?" Kenisha whispered.

Oh, God. Kenisha. I turned my head to look at her. "Hey, Kenisha. I'm so sorry. Did we wake you?"

"That's OK." She ventured into the kitchen. "Is everything alright?"

"Be awfully careful. There's broken glass all over." I sighed deeply. My house must seem as bad as her own. Or worse.

"I just get so frustrated sometimes. I lost my temper." Poor thing didn't need to hear my troubles. "What can I get you for breakfast?"

"I can fix it myself." She came closer and put her hand on my shoulder. "My momma yells at Calvin like that sometimes. She just wants him to be good. They still love each other. You and Jack, too." She patted me.

I had to wonder. Kenisha got the broom and started to clean up the mess. I excused myself and took refuge in my bedroom. I found the yellow pages in the phone book and started looking under T for "therapists". It was difficult to see through the tears.

Later in the morning I felt the need to get out of the house, but I didn't want to go anyplace. I walked over and tapped on Howard's front door.

"Come in, come in." Howard's thin white hair stood on end and his black-framed glasses hung from the end of his nose.

"You busy?"

"Naw. Just looking out at my feeders. I've got a couple of cardinals and a squirrel, is all. For you I've got all the time in the world. Come on in and have a seat. Can I fix you a cup of tea or something? I've got some of that Russian tea mix. That's good. Sort of spicy."

"Sounds nice. I'll have some of that."

Howard busied himself in the kitchen and I looked around his living room. I'd never been inside his house before. We were "yard" friends, so I was surprised to see the room furnished and decorated with beautiful and sophisticated furniture and art. Dusty, but beautiful. A display cabinet showed off a collection of beautiful handmade dolls that looked Oriental. An overflowing bookcase was stuffed with paperback mysteries, current novels in hardback, and Shelby Foote's three volume Civil War series.

He had 'worked for the government' he'd told me, retiring several years ago. I suspected the CIA or FBI. He revealed little about himself except that there were a couple of sons who lived far away and visited only occasionally. An average looking guy with regular features, Howard could easily go unnoticed in a crowd. Like a spy. Or was I making that up?

"Are you a Civil War buff?" I asked when he returned with our tea. I noticed that he had smoothed his hair and removed the eyeglasses.

"Oh, I got turned on by the Ken Burns TV documentary. I loved to hear Shelby Foote say 'the Civil Waw-wah'. I found those books at an estate sale. I might read them sometime." As he put a cup of tea on the table at my elbow, I noticed his hands. Long, strong fingers, square-cut nails. Mother would have approved. He settled into a recliner, his cup on the arm.

"And tell me about your doll collection. You don't strike me as a doll person."

"Those were my wife's. I got them for her in Thailand. They are called Hill Tribe dolls, and are made in the little villages there. She loved them."

I didn't ask, but after a moment he provided the answer. "Irma died seven years ago. Cancer."

"I'm so sorry, Howard."

"Well, you know cancer," he replied. "She was ill for nearly five years. By the time she died I was just happy her suffering was over. But I do miss her a lot."

I tasted the tea. Hot. Spicy. Good. We sat quietly with our own thoughts for a few minutes.

"The reason I came over was to tell you about my new house guest."

"Well, I have to admit I've been a little curious."

I told him about Kenisha. Where I'd met her and the con she'd pulled on me. And about Calvin and her mother, and Jerome and Tasha. And why she was staying with me. "She'll go home after the baby comes."

"That's awfully kind of you, Roberta, but isn't it a big responsibility?"

"I know. But I feel drawn to this kid for some reason. She's got such great potential and so few resources to draw on. Maybe it's because I failed so badly with Jack."

Howard looked at me quizzically.

"Actually, he just got out of prison. I never told you that. He tried to rob a bank eight years ago."

There, I'd said it. Howard didn't act shocked or even surprised so I pushed on. "He had a drug and alcohol problem and he needed lots of money so that was his solution. But he's got a job now, and I think he's going to be OK. I hope so, anyhow."

"That's good. I'll help you hope." His smile was comforting, but there was a wariness in his eyes that I didn't understand. "If there's anything I can do, Roberta, let me know. I've had a little experience with people with that problem." His sincerity was evident but he didn't elaborate.

We returned to talking about Kenisha. "At first I wanted her to give up the baby, but she'll not even consider it. And who am I to be telling her that anyway? The girls in the projects think it is the only way to have someone love you unconditionally. Huh! She may be right."

"I had a daughter," Howard said softly. His eyes had a far-away look.

I sat silent, surprised, waiting. He cleared his throat. A dam seemed to open.

"I had a daughter," he repeated. "Laura. I can't tell you how much I loved that child." Anguish sculpted his face.

I was startled. "Howard? What happened?"

"It was the drugs. She got caught up in all of that and it killed her." He buried his face in his hands, his shoulders shaking.

What had I done? I knelt by his side, and put my hand on his shoulder. "I'm sorry, Howard. So sorry. What can I do?"

"Be happy you still have Jack, Roberta. That's what you can do. Now just go away. I need to be by myself." He pulled away from me.

I tiptoed out of his house and went home. Like our backyards, our secrets are hidden from view. Having shared our secrets, Howard and I, I wondered if our friendship would survive.

***

When Jack came home I apologized profusely for my terrible temper tantrum. He was sullen, but gruffed out, "That's OK, Mom. I know you freak about money. I'll pay you back, just give me time."

I tried to hug him, but he squirmed out of my embrace and walked away, calling, "Here, kitty, kitty." When the cats came prancing to him he gathered them up and went into his room, closing the door.

Chapter 13

The phone book listed several therapists and I picked at random. When I called for an appointment at one, I was told she was taking no new patients at the present time. Call back in six months. I knew I couldn't wait that long.

I was able to see another, a Doctor Phillips, on short notice. His offices were elaborate, furnished with heavy brocaded chairs, a matching sofa and love seat and mahogany tables. The walls were a dark green, and expensive looking window treatments said 'big bucks'. The reception room was empty and I only had a short wait before the doctor would see me. I knew it was a mistake the minute I walked in and saw the man behind the desk. He looked like he was costumed for the part of a New York psychiatrist in a play from the 1920's; a high collar, formal morning coat, even a pince-nez hanging from a chain attached to his lapel. I couldn't believe it. He looked as out of place in Midsouth City as a Laplander in Texas.

"I'm sorry. There's been a mistake," I said and backed out the door. There was no way I could ever feel comfortable talking about my problems with that man. I hardly made it to my car before I burst out laughing. Talk about crazy!

I couldn't give up though, so hoping for the best, I tried yet another therapist from the phone book. They could 'squeeze' me in, the woman on the phone said, and gave me an appointment for the following week.

'Family Therapy, Dr. Lloyd Fitzwater' said the sign on the door. The waiting room was unimpressive, a far cry from Dr. Phillip's office. Orange plastic chairs lined the walls, and a children's play area dominated one corner. A few old and tattered magazines littered a couple of small tables and made me wonder if I was in the right place. The receptionist confirmed my appointment, however, and said yes, the doctor would see me soon. I claimed one of the orange chairs and tried to settle in.

A mother with a young child waited, too. The boy was tossing building blocks around recklessly. One conked me on the head. The mother said, "Donny, darling, tell the lady you're sorry." He ignored her. I ignored them, and soon they were called in to see the doctor.

While I waited I could feel my nerves. My stomach fluttered and my one knee jiggled. I'd guarded my secrets for so long I wondered how I could relate them to a perfect stranger. Of course, maybe that was the point. I was practicing my opening lines when Donny and his mommy finally returned, neither of them looking happy. A nurse came and ushered me into the inner sanctum.

The doctor looked about 15, and very laid back, wearing a ponytail, worn jeans, a pink, open collared shirt under a tweed sport coat, and rimless glasses like my granny used to wear. His office was furnished somewhat better than the reception room, with walls painted a soothing gray/green. Dark upholstered chairs were arranged in a conversational grouping around a glass topped coffee table littered with books and magazines. The windows were draped nicely, and framed black and white photographs on one wall featured the faces, just the faces, of individuals from many stages of life. I walked over to examine them. A wrinkled old man smoking a pipe. A serene young woman. A tiny baby sound asleep. A grinning freckle-faced boy in a baseball cap. The room had a homey, comfortable feeling.

I checked the wall behind his desk for the obligatory framed degrees and diplomas that would give a boost to my confidence in his ability to diagnose my problem. My glasses were in my purse, so I couldn't make out the details, but there seemed to be an impressive number. He watched as I inspected his office, but didn't say anything.

When I was ready he stood and we introduced ourselves. He invited me to sit and came from behind his paper laden desk and sat facing me. He didn't look quite as young as I'd first thought. He was clean shaven except for a bushy mustache and I think I detected a few gray hairs there. His eyes were an interesting mixture of browns and greens. Not exactly piercing, but keen.

"How can I help you today, Ms. Fischer?"

"Well, I don't know if you can. You see, it's my son. I'm afraid I'm going to kill him." I gasped, clapping my hand over my mouth. "Goodness! That isn't what I meant to say."

"And why would you do that – kill him, I mean?" His kind eyes looked directly into mine. I had his attention, but he didn't look the least bit shocked. I suppose he'd heard worse, but what could be worse than murder?

"Because I get so angry." My lower lip quivered and I pushed back tears.

"Ah." There was a long pause. Finally he prompted me, gently. "Can you describe your anger? How it feels to you?" He tipped his head to one side and leaned forward, looking totally absorbed.

"Well. It lies there, just below the surface, festering, festering…. then erupts like a volcano; a giant out of control. It grips me tight and my brain goes blank. It's scary."

"I see. And what sets it off, do you know?" He sat back, but his eyes never left mine.

"Hmmm. Well, I guess the short answer is that Jack, my son, is just out of prison and living at my house. He's driving me crazy and then I get mad and lose my temper."

"I see. And the long answer?"

I thought a while. "It started a long time ago, when he was still a child and has been going on ever since."

The man was into long pauses, I'll say that. But it made me feel as if he weren't just following a script; that he was sorting through my feelings and my needs, and how best to meet them.

"Alright then. Let's start there. Is it alright with you if I record this? It will help me get to know you and Jack both a bit better if I can re-play our sessions."

I gave my assent, and he pushed a button on a small recorder on the table in front him.

"Thank you. Now go ahead. Tell me a little about your family and about Jack's childhood." He sat back in his chair again, his legs crossed, relaxed but attentive.

And so I did, starting with the fact that we adopted him when he was four months old. I told him about Steve and our life in the Army and when we first started noticing that Jack seemed a bit different than the other children. The doctor listened carefully, asked a question now and then, and took occasional notes. Very soon our time was up. I had just scratched the surface.

"What I'd like you to do, Ms. Fischer, is to start writing down some of the things you remember about Jack's behavior. And look for patterns, things he did repeatedly that bothered you. Next week I want to go over a list of questions I have that may help you recall some of his actions. Ones you may have forgotten about. Once we have those identified, then I think we can begin to look at your reactions and begin to understand why you respond the way you do. And maybe prevent a murder." His lips quirked at one corner, but quickly became serious. "In the meantime, if you start to lose your temper, try just walking away. Leave the house, if you must. And call me if you want to. How does that sound to you?"

"It's just so nice to unload all this stuff, Doctor. I feel better already. But could you just call me Roberta?"

"Of course, Roberta."

"Thanks. I'll see you next week, then."

Afterwards, I reported by phone to Julie, admitting I'd gone for help with my anger. "But Julie, I'm in love!"

"You mean with Dan?"

"Well, maybe. But, no, with this new doctor. He's the cutest, smartest kid you have ever seen. Well, not actually a kid. He's, uh, oh twenty four if he's a day."

She laughed. "That old, huh? He must be a prodigy."

"And the best part? I get to see him again. Next week. I can hardly wait."

"My mother used to say, 'there's no fool like an old fool'. I'm beginning to see what she was talking about. Other than being in love, do you think he might be able to help you?"

"Oh, spoil sport. Of course. That's the best part. I really think he can."

And so began my weekly visits to Dr. Fitzwater. The inventory of Jack's childhood behaviors was revealing, both to the doctor and to me. Viewing them from the distance of time I could see a pattern emerge that began to look ominous, even to me. Lying, cheating, stealing. Lack of conscience. Total inability to manage even his weekly allowance. And as he grew older, when drugs and alcohol were introduced, well, the list went on….and on. When Dr. Fitz mentioned the possibility of a personality disorder I went to the library and asked for help finding information on the subject.

I learned about things like paranoia, schizophrenia, bi-polar and antisocial behavior. Of all the symptoms listed in all of the personality disorders I read about, I could readily identify at least three that Jack displayed quite vividly. First was his addiction to both drugs and alcohol. Second was his inability to manage money. And third was 'splitting', as Dr. Fitzwater had pointed out.

Jack often idealized people on first meeting, only to vilify them later. I also suspected him to be bi-polar as his mood swings were sometimes quite dramatic. What a fool I'd been, to ignore Julie's offers of information, and to think that I could solve something that was unsolvable, at least by an uninformed mother.

Emerging, also, were the patterns of my reactions to Jack's behavior. When the doctor led me to recognize that my pride was wounded, I refused to admit it. Me? Prideful? I'd never thought that of myself.

"How did you feel when Jack's picture appeared in the newspaper and on TV when he was caught robbing the bank?" The doc pulled no punches.

"Oh. Well, embarrassed to tears, naturally. Here I was, a well-known non-profit executive, officer in the Rotary Club, member of the United Way Board of Directors, with a bank robber, well, alleged bank robber, for a son. He was the lead story that day, both in the paper and on the evening TV news."

A long pause. The good doctor just sat there, watching me.

Finally, "Ah, yes, I see what you mean. 'Pride goeth before the fall'". Oh, dear. Self-recognition could be so hard.

And so it went over the next weeks and months. It was uncomfortable to look at, much less discuss, my feelings of guilt, anger, and resentment because my image of myself was of a nice, good hearted person. I'd heard it said that everyone has a dark side, but surely that did not apply to me. Did it?

I called Dan to apologize for falling asleep after our dinner. "I'm sorry," I said. "It's just that between Jack and Kenisha I'm awfully busy and I just get tired."

"I can see that, Roberta," he replied. "You know, I think you've bitten off more than you can chew for your age."

My age? Humph!

"Can't you send the girl home, and get Jack to move out? That way you could have more time, wouldn't get so tired, and maybe we could take that trip together."

I looked at the phone in my hand for a long minute, then quietly hung up. As the receiver went down I could hear Dan saying, "Hello? Roberta?"

Standing at the stove simmering soup for supper, I almost missed the faint knock at the back door. "Howard?"

"Hi, Roberta." He stood there with his head down, hat in hand, the picture of dejection. "I just came to apologize for that little scene at my house. You have enough problems without me weighing you down with mine."

I called to Kenisha to come dish up the soup and stepped outside.

"Now you listen to me, Howard." I laid my hand on his shoulder and made him look me in the eye. "You have nothing to apologize for. You're grieving. It's the human thing to do. You've boxed your grief away, and that's alright. Except every once in a while you have to un-box it, look at it, feel it, and deal with it. Like cry, get angry, kick something." It was almost exactly what Dr. Fitzwater told me to do with my anger.

"Kick something?" He almost chuckled.

"Does wonders." I hugged him. "Why don't you come in and have some soup with me and Kenisha? That does wonders, too."

We sat around the kitchen table, eating my good homemade vegetable soup, passing around the crackers and cheese. Kenisha entertained with stories from the projects. Howard countered with some of his adventures in India and Africa and Thailand. Turns out he had worked for the U. S. Agency for International Development (USAID). I listened, and laughed, and kept the bowls full. I also suggested that perhaps he'd like to help us fix up Kenisha's apartment. He could paint with Jerome while Julie and I washed windows and cleaned up in general.

"I could do that," he said. He grinned at Kenisha and squeezed her hand where it lay on the table. "What do you want? Purple? Fuschia?"

Chapter 14

One evening a couple of weeks later Kenisha went to bed early after talking to Jerome and her aunt and Tasha. She talked to them every day, but didn't ask to go home again. I was happy to have her here, far from Calvin, and safe with me.

I was getting ready for bed when Jack came in. "I'm hungry. Have you got any meat I can cook?" He avoided looking at me.

"There are some pork chops in the fridge. You can have a couple of them if you like." Was he acting a bit strange? "Just broil them in the toaster oven."

"I know. I know. You don't have to tell me everything."

"I'm going on to bed, then. Good night."

Sleep eluded me as the aroma of grilling pork chops teased me. When the odors strengthened from teasing to taunting I thought it strange and decided to check. Jack's bedroom door stood wide open, lights on. He lay face down across the bed, unmoving. Startled, I followed my nose to the kitchen, barefooted, wearing only my nylon nightgown.

The pork chops were ablaze. Flames and smoke fingered their way around the toaster oven door and reached for the cupboard above. I snatched open a drawer and grabbed a potholder. Flipping open the door, I reached in and seized the sizzling pan. It fell with a clatter on the counter top, splashing bits of burning grease on the counter and down to the floor. One of the charred pieces of pork fell into the open drawer and smoldered there among the dish cloths. I picked up the still flaming pan and threw it behind me into the sink. Water from the faucet splashed the flames into submission.

Turning back I found the fire spreading rapidly. The counter, the cupboards above, the drawer below, all engaged. Hot grease blistered my feet and heat forced me backwards.

"Jack! Jack!" I yelled. I needed help.

Smoke was thickening, and the alarm in the hall started to shrill. Still no sign of Jack. I opened my mouth to shout for Kenisha when she appeared in the doorway.

She was holding a towel between her legs "Mz. Fischer? I hate to bother you, but I think my water broke."

Oh, my God. Fire was taking over the kitchen. I abandoned my efforts to stop it.

I put my arm around Kenisha and inched with her back to her room. "Let's get your hospital suitcase and get outdoors. We'll use the front door." I dialed 911 from the phone on her desk with one hand while helping her pull a coat around her shoulders with the other.

"And hurry!" I banged the phone down.

The smell of smoke grew stronger. "Come on, now. We have to get outside."

"I can't find Tigger and Patches. They were here with me but I don't see them now." A quick search of the room revealed nothing.

"Come on, now. We've got to go."

Kenisha was on her hands and knees, looking under the bed and calling, "Here, Kitty, Kitty. Here, Kitty, Kitty."

"Kenisha, honey, you're about to have a baby. The fire is spreading and you've gotta get out." As I ushered her out the front door I assured her, "I'll be right behind you with Jack and the kittens. And when the ambulance comes, go to it and tell them your water broke. They'll take care of you."

Limping back down the hall I screamed again. "Jack! Jack! Get up. The house is on fire."

I detoured into my bedroom and shoved my feet into some shoes. Strings of smoke were threading through the house. I pulled a sweater on and staggered back to Jack. I knew I couldn't lift him so I tried to drag him. I took hold of a corner of the bedspread and heaved. Nothing. I dug in my heels and heaved again. Slowly the body moved, but only a few inches. I could hear sirens in the distance. At last, after a final desperate tug he fell to the floor and I could slide him easily across the hardwood. Once we got to the carpeted hallway though, we stuck. Smoke filled the house now. I was coughing and choking. I had to get out but I couldn't bear to leave Jack behind. I stood there, frozen between choices.

From somewhere deep inside me emerged the absolute conviction that, just as I could not bear to think of my son living under a bridge, neither could I bear to abandon him here in my burning home.

Gritting my teeth I called for an extra burst of adrenaline and began pulling at Jack again, this time by his ankles. He started to paddle his foot at me in annoyance and mumbled, "Quit it. What are you doing? Leave me alone."

"The house is on fire, Jack. You have to get up and we have to get out. I can't pull you anymore. Come on. Crawl."

That finally got his attention. He elbowed around into a crawling position and, following me, started for the front door. "What happened? What's burning?"

"Pork chops," was all I could manage.

Flames were visible in the dining room eating at my window treatments. Heat from the fire was building. We were nearly to the front door when I remembered the kittens.

"You go on, Jack. I'll be right behind you. I have to get Tigger and Patches."

Jack seemed fully alert now. "I'll get them, Mom." Without another word he turned around and crawled back down the hall.

When I opened the front door there was the most beautiful sight I've ever seen; fire fighters fitting themselves out in goggles and air packs. One of them reached in and pulled me out the door and onto the grass while the others filed into the house.

"My son. Looking for kittens. Down the hall." I choked out.

Fire trucks, an ambulance and police cars lined the street. Red and blue revolving lights spiraled the scene into a disco setting. Neighbors crowded along the sidewalk, their faces a kaleidoscope. I could see the Newberrys and the Barrs looking on in horror.

"Where's Kenisha?" I asked of my rescuer, oblivious to the chaos.

"The pregnant girl? They've taken her to the hospital already."

"Is anyone with her?"

"She's got two paramedics with her, ma'am. She's doing fine."

They sat me down and tried to clamp an oxygen mask to my face. I waved them away, struggled up and back toward the house. "Jack. Have they found Jack?" I couldn't take my eyes off the front door, hoping for a glimpse of him.

Howard broke through the spectators and came to stand beside me. "Roberta? Are you alright?"

"They're looking for Jack and the kittens, but I have to get to the hospital, Howard. I have to be there for Kenisha. I brought her here to be safe. Is this safe? Just look, is this safe?" I swept my hand toward the burning house.

"Honey, I saw Kenisha when she came out. There are people with her, and she can call her family when she gets to the hospital. She'll be OK."

Howard put an arm around me. It was comforting, but I pulled away, keeping my eyes on the front door and praying for Jack.

At first fire ballooned from the kitchen windows. But torrents of water from the firemen's hoses tamed those flames and slowly the fire came under control. My little home oozed smoke and dripped water. It smelled acrid and ugly. A hole had been chopped in the roof, and shards of glass littered the ground beneath the windows.

It seemed like an eternity before two firemen emerged from the front door supporting Jack between them. A third fireman followed holding a kitty in his arms. The crowd clapped. Jack was loaded onto a gurney and into the remaining ambulance where the paramedics took over.

Howard walked forward and took the kitty from the fireman. After a brief conversation he came back. "They could only find one," he said. It was Tigger. "I'll take care of him, Roberta. Don't worry, he'll be fine." I burst into tears. Poor Patches. How could I ever tell Kenisha? She had loved him so much.

Someone helped me into the ambulance where Jack was sitting up, looking confused behind an oxygen mask. The doors slammed shut and we started to move. For the first time I looked down. My nightgown had melted and beneath the sweater only my white cotton panties showed. A kindly paramedic spread a sheet around me, and slipped an oxygen mask over my face.

The siren sounded shrill in the night, but I was beginning to feel pain in my hands and feet and I was glad for the ride.

Howard arrived at the hospital soon after I did and sat in the waiting room while I was being treated. He stuck his head into the cubicle once to inform me that Jack had been admitted and he'd find out his room number. "I left Tigger with Mrs. Markowitz. She owns a bunch of cats so it's no problem and she's pleased she can help."

I signaled to the nurse working over me to remove the oxygen mask for a moment. "See if you can find out about Kenisha too, will you?" I asked Howard, my voice reduced to a rough whisper. "And call Julie ..tell what happened … ask her to bring me … clothes. Please." The effort exhausted me. "Julie Gilbert… on Madison… in the book."

They shot me full of morphine and worked a long time cleaning and pulling glass from my feet and hands. The pain was intense at times, even through the morphine. I finally fell asleep. When I came to it was morning and I found myself alone in a room with my hands and feet heavily bandaged, and with oxygen tubes up my nose. A nurse came in and helped me use a bed pan and later an aide came and gave me a bath. I was trying to figure out how to eat the breakfast they'd delivered when Julie stuck her head in the door.

"Oh, you're awake. Good!" she said. "I brought you some clothes." She squished toward me across the tile floor in her red high-tops, putting down her purse and a paper bag on the way.

"Howard made me go home last night after we knew you were OK, but he stayed. Is he still here?"

"Howard?" My voice came out in a croak.

"Yeah, I think he spent most of the night."

"Haven't seen him. You know anything ... Jack?" My throat and lungs hurt with the effort to speak.

Julie pulled a chair close to the bed and sat down. "Jack's on another ward. I wrote his room number down. You can call him, I think."

"Kenisha?"

"Let's call and find out." Julie picked up the phone and after a few inquiries held the phone to my ear.

"Mz. Fischer?"

"Kenisha?"

"I had the baby, Mz. Fischer. It was hard but I did OK. Are you alright? You sound funny."

I surprised myself by bursting into tears. Julie reclaimed the phone.

"She's going to be OK, but her throat hurts from all that smoke," Julie assured her. "It might be a day or two until she can come visit you."

They talked some more and I could see from the smile on Julie's face that Kenisha was doing well, and that the baby was perfect.

When she hung up Julie reported. "That's where Howard's been. Apparently he hopped back and forth between here and Jack's room and the maternity ward, and was there when the baby came. Kenisha said to tell you that he's gone home now, but will be back later. Jerome and her aunt and even her mother are up there with her. She's anxious for you to come see her and the baby, too, of course."

Julie fed me my breakfast but I fell asleep halfway through the applesauce. When I woke up she was gone, and Howard sat dozing in the chair beside my bed, a book in his lap. He looked tired, but was clean shaven and had on fresh clothes.

I chuckled out loud when I saw the book; Shelby Foote's 'Civil War, Volume I'.

He jerked awake. Looking abashed he said, "Well, I thought this would be as good a time as any to read old Shelby." Recovering, he added, "It's nice to see you awake and smiling. How are you doing?"

I waved my bandaged hands at him, and wiggled my bandaged feet. "Other than a few cuts and burns, I'm OK, I think." My voice still sounded like gravel in a grinder. "I haven't seen the doctor yet today, though." I coughed. "Sorry."

Just then a nurse knocked and came in leaving the door wide open. She started to cut away my bandages. "The doctor is on his way and will want to look at your wounds." She looked at Howard. "You can stay if you wish, Mr. Fischer, or wait in the hall if you'd rather. We need to move that chair so the doctor can examine her."

Howard didn't point out her error, but tucked his book under his arm, shoved the chair away from the bed and, retreating to a corner replied, "I'll stay."

She finished just as a doctor swept in like a ship under sail on the open sea. He took my chart from the nurse and glanced at it, then peered at my hands and feet. He announced, "I'm Doctor Gillespie, Mrs. Fischer. Your hands and feet have 1st and 2nd degree burns and some cuts. They will be painful, but if treated properly should heal in a few weeks.

"More serious is the fact that you inhaled a lot of smoke. Because of the danger of damage to your lungs and the possibility of pneumonia we're going to keep you here for a few days. I'm starting you on an IV of antibiotics to fight infection, and also keeping you on oxygen." He glanced at Howard and made the same mistake as the nurse. "When she comes home you'll need to put on fresh dressings a couple of times a day, but she'll be fine in a few weeks." He patted my shoulder and after a brief consultation with the nurse sailed away again, a ship with many ports of call to make.

The nurse slathered my feet and hands with salve and put on fresh bandages, and a technician arrived to set up my IV. Howard left to check on Jack. I was more worried about him than I was about myself. What was to become of us? We had no home to return to, I needed nursing care, and I didn't even know what Jack's needs would be.

I was alone again and weeping quietly when Howard returned.

He moved the chair back beside my bed, and using a tissue gently mopped the tears from my face. "It's going to be OK. Don't cry."

"Jack?" I croaked.

"He's not injured, just suffering from smoke inhalation like you. They're going to keep him a few days, too. They did a tox screen and found heroin and some marijuana, but nothing else. It wasn't an overdose, he was just high."

Just high? All this, and he was 'just high'? It was not exactly how I expected to spend the day that Kenisha's baby was born. That should have been another kind of high, the good kind, the 'whoopee the pain's over and now we have a new baby to love' kind of high. I hate to use an obscenity, but sometimes life *is* a bitch.

The next day an aide brought Jack to visit me. He, too, had oxygen tubes up his nose and a tank hanging on a hook at the back of the wheelchair. Boney, freckled hands clamped the hospital gown to his knees. He looked at my bandaged hands and feet. "I'm sorry, Mom. I'm really sorry."

"Oh, Jack." I was speechless. Never before in our lives had I heard an apology from him. Now was not the time to confront him about his drug use and I had no idea where we were going to live when we were released from the hospital. "I don't know what we're going to do." My lower lip quivered as I tried to hold myself together.

Jack rolled himself closer to my bed.

"They had a social worker come talk to me. I guess I was pretty high that night so they want to send me to Rehab." Jack was more subdued than I'd ever seen him and for once his blue eyes looked directly into mine. "Is the house really gone?"

"As good as gone. Howard says the damage is pretty extensive and it will take months to get it ready to live in again."

"If I go to Rehab, where will you go?" That's the first time I can ever remember Jack asking after my well-being.

"I might be able to stay with Julie. Her place is small, but we can probably make do for a while."

"OK, then." Predictably he added, "I'm going to need some new clothes, though." He patted my arm and then as if he'd solved the world's problems he signaled the aide, who rolled him away down the hall.

I couldn't wait to see Kenisha and the baby. That afternoon Jerome and Myra showed up at my door pushing an empty wheelchair. They carefully loaded me in, hooked up my oxygen tank and we set off for the maternity ward. I was as excited as if I were a kid going to see Santa for the very first time.

The baby was visiting her mother when we arrived. Kenisha looked worn out, but her face was beaming. "Oh, Mz. Fischer. Come look!" She turned the baby toward me. "Isn't she beautiful?"

She was beautiful. With a soft knit cap on her head and the rest of her all bundled up only her little face was visible. Her eyes were closed tight, her mouth working frantically. One tiny fist broke free and beat at the air. Kenisha pulled her to her breast. She had found her 'something to love that will love you back.'

With an admiring audience of Myra on one side of her bed and me on the other and while Jerome stood grinning at the foot of the bed, Kenisha said, "Guess what her name is." Myra and I shook our heads.

"Lolo Roberta Myra Johnson," Kenisha announced proudly.

Myra and I broke out in delighted laughter. "Poor baby," I said.

A nurse put her head in the door. "Shhh, you're disturbing the other patients."

We put a lid on our celebration, but it didn't diminish our joy.

Chapter 15

It took a while to sort it all out, but finally Jack went to rehab for a few months while Julie took me in. I slept on a rollaway bed in her living room, dozing off and on during the day. A home health worker came every day for about a week to tend to my feet and hands. Some afternoons Myra brought Kenisha and Lolo to visit me. Other times 'Movie Mary' showed up with a video and we watched a movie. Once I even looked in Julie's bedroom closet and discovered her collection of red, high-top tennis shoes. There were three: one pair well worn, one shabby and very well worn, and one pair still in the box, brand new. And one pair of black pumps I'd never seen her wear. When Julie came home from work (wearing still another pair of red sneakers) we ate take-out then listened to music, played cards and visited.

Howard often joined us in the evenings and helped me through the insurance maze and blueprints for the renovation. He kept me apprised of our bird feeder population and continued to provide a home for Tigger with help from Mrs. Marcowitz when he needed it. He also agreed to keep an eye on the work at my house when it started. Dan even came to visit me, bringing another super market bouquet. Howard was there at the time and they eyed each other with suspicion. Dan didn't stay long, and promised to come back, but he never did.

Julie's comment was, "My Lord, Bertie, for someone who claims to be a dried up prune, you seem to be attracting flies like a ripe plum."

"Or a rotten one," I corrected, smiling and pumping my eyebrows up and down, hoping for a Groucho Marx effect.

Kenisha went back to Roosevelt where the ladies of the project hovered, Jerome took on the 'man of the house' role, and Calvin mostly stayed away. Myra kept close tabs on her. Kenisha and I talked on the phone every day so I kept up on her motherhood, and she kept up on me. She, too, mourned the loss of Patches, but she had another little one to love, now. Little 'Lolo Roberta Myra Johnson' had her full attention. There was no more mention of school and I didn't have the energy to pursue the subject.

Repair work began on my house and would take several months to complete. I was grateful for the insurance I had been paying into for so many years as it covered almost everything. When my feet healed enough I stopped by every day to check on the work. One or another of my neighbors would come by to check things out as well. Bill Newberry for one, although Phyllis never showed her face. And Jenna and her husband Jim.

Often Howard came over, too, and we inspected things together and made sure my bird feeders were kept full. Afterward we'd drift back to his house where we might have a drink, talk birds, and occasionally he'd fix us something to eat. His specialty was Thai food. What he could do with a mango was magical. It's a staple of Thai food he said. When I admitted I'd never even bought a mango he explained that he and his family had lived in Thailand for a number of years when his work was centered there. Which also accounted for the beautiful Thai furniture and art work displayed around his home.

I discovered other surprising things about Howard, too. One evening he invited me to come to the back of his house, to a large windowed room with hardwood floors overlooking the back yard. Sparsely furnished, it housed a treadmill and stationary bicycle, and a rack with weights. An old-fashioned record player rested on a table in one corner.

'I've been wanting to ask you to dance for a long time. Do you think your feet can take it?"

"Oh!" I looked with new eyes at this seemingly quiet, bookish gentleman. "Well, let's find out. I haven't danced in years but I'm willing to give it a try."

Howard moved the exercise equipment to one side. "Glenn Miller?" he asked. At my enthusiastic "Wonderful!" he selected a record from his obviously extensive collection on a shelf nearby and put it on the turntable. He turned, held out a hand and pulled me to him as the strains of 'In the Mood' filled the room. As if we'd danced many times before we melded together and moved almost as one. I was a bit rusty, but all those years of dancing at the Officers' Clubs at army bases from Georgia and North Carolina to Iceland, soon paid off. Howard proved to be an excellent dancer. It was fun. A two-step, a tango, a waltz, and yes, even the Twist. And, of course, many sit-downs between songs to rest a bit. At last we staggered back to the living room and collapsed on the couch, winded, but laughing.

As I was getting ready to go back to Julie's we hugged at the door as usual. Then Howard pulled me closer. "I wish you wouldn't go. Stay with me tonight." He kissed me, and not on the cheek. In my brain I was astonished, but the rest of me responded, feeling quite at home in his embrace. Some other feelings surfaced, too. Feelings I hadn't had in many years. That first kiss led to others, longer, deeper, sweeter.

"But Julie is expecting me........."

"Call her."

I dialed Julie and he took the phone from my hand. When Julie answered he said, "Berta's staying over here tonight. She'll call you tomorrow." Without waiting for an answer he hung up.

"Rotten plum, my eye," Julie chided when I called her the next day.

"Oh, my." I tried to think of a snappy retort, but failed.

"You're grinning! I can hear you grinning." Julie's chortle was infectious and I could almost see her in her red shoes, dancing up and down with delight.

***

In December I celebrated with two parties in my newly renovated digs. The first, early in the month, was for my neighbors who were eager to see the inside of the house they'd been watching for so long as it was rebuilt. Even Phyllis came, her hair out of curlers and dressed in a nice skirt and blouse. She didn't say much, but she didn't miss much either, looking curiously into every room. Mrs. Marcowitz arrived with a gift; a young kitten she explained had been Tigger's special friend when he was staying at her house. "They always do better when there are at least two," she explained. It was obvious to see that Tigger thought so, too.

Bobby Ortiz spent the afternoon on the floor with the cats. At first his dad shyly visited with just Bill Newberry and Jim Barr. But Howard acted as the genial host and soon had everyone chatting with neighbors they'd only waved at in passing before. And everyone revealed things about themselves we hadn't known. The Candolis from across the street were related to the famous Trip Candoli who played trumpet in some of the greatest bands of the 50's and 60's. Quiet Mr. Newberry had been present when the first atomic bomb was detonated at White Sands in New Mexico. The Barrs had been missionaries in South America. Most surprising however was Mr. Ortiz. He moved here from Mexico where he had been an architect but was working as a master plumber now. Even Phyllis seemed impressed.

I think this was the first time all these neighbors had come together and it occurred to me that a bit of détente was taking place. Not a bad thing. I was pleased that out of my misfortune some good had come.

The second was a Christmas party for my 'family'. Even Jack was there. He was home from Rehab and seemed happy to be back. We'd had to go clothes shopping again, but this time we hit the Salvation Army and Goodwill stores. I'd even found some badly needed things for myself.

Myra, looking smart as always in a red and green tunic over black tights, brought a van load of people; Kenisha and Lolo, Tasha and her baby Michael, and

Jerome as well as Auntie Gloria Swanson. I put out sandwiches, nibbles and soft drinks and Howard contributed a huge sheet cake decorated with a happy Santa Claus. Julie (wearing brand new red tennies, I swear it) brought chips and dip. Everyone helped themselves. The babble rose in volume, or dropped to a murmur depending on the moods of Lolo and Mikey.

We took turns holding the babies and Jerome and Howard retreated to a corner to talk man-stuff with Jack lurking nearby. They all took their turns, too, at playing with the little ones and Tigger, especially Jack who seemed most comfortable in their company.

As the party was winding down, Kenisha came back from 'her' room where she had been changing a diaper on Lolo. "Mz. Fischer, I just noticed how big your room is now with a big new bathroom and all. That's really nice." She gave me a quizzical look.

Howard and I looked at each other. "Shall we?" I said.

He gave a slight nod and came to stand by me, putting his arm around me. "Yes, well we have a little announcement to make….." he said, grinning.

***

We were married on Valentine's Day. Jack stood up with Howard and Julie was my matron of honor. We honeymooned on a 3 day Caribbean Cruise featuring a golden oldies dance band.

Howard sold his house and moved over to mine where we made room for us all with a large new addition that took up about 1/3 of the back yard. There were rooms for Jack and Kenisha when she was there with Lolo as well as a large suite for me and Howard.

Howard and I settled into married life, enjoying our home and our friends. Dances at the Elks Club were high on our list of entertainment and we joined a Bird Club and spent many Saturday's exploring the back roads, swamps and woods in the area for species never seen at back yard feeders.

Chapter 16

Jack, after his months in rehab, was staying off of drugs and alcohol but his behavior was often bizarre. For a while he was friendly with Howard and praised him often for being 'a really cool dude'.

One day, though, he came to me in the kitchen while I was fixing dinner.

Without preamble he growled, "That Howard's an asshole."

The cooking spoon in my hand fell to the floor. "What?"

"You heard me. I said Howard's an asshole."

I picked up the spoon and slumped onto a chair at the kitchen table. "But you like Howard." I stared at Jack, not believing what I was hearing.

"I never liked Howard. He's just using you to get a nicer house and someone to wait on him. You've been screwed. Yeah, Mom, screwed." He dragged the word out lasciviously. His dirty laugh and nasty leer tripped the trigger of my anger. I exploded.

"Get out!" I screamed, leaping out of the chair. "Just get the hell out of my house and stay out!" Using the long cooking spoon I started beating him on the head and shoulders and continued screaming, just curse words now. He wrapped his arms around his head and, still laughing, retreated toward the hallway.

Howard came into the kitchen, grabbed Jack and pushed him down the hall. Then he wrapped his arms around me. "Hush, now. Calm down. Hush. Hush."

He rocked me in his arms until my fury subsided and continued holding me as I sobbed.

The black dog returned that night after a long absence, growling and snarling and rattling his chain. As I tried to run away, Howard shook me awake and held me close until I fell asleep again.

"Where's Jack?" were my first words in the morning. Howard was already up and dressed, and carrying a steaming cup of coffee to me as I sat up. It had been a long, tough night and I felt lousy.

"In his room. I've talked to him and we're OK for now." Howard sat on the bed beside me and pushed the hair away from my face. "I've called Dr. Fitzwater and he will see us before office hours this morning. You need to get up and in the shower. We'll leave as soon as you're ready."

I didn't argue. My outburst and tirade had frightened me and I knew I needed help as much as Jack did. Howard was being a saint, but would he decide I wasn't worth keeping after all? I couldn't bear the thought.

Dr. Fitzwater opened the office door himself. "My staff won't be here for a few more minutes, come on in." He showed us into his private office. "What's going on?" he asked as we seated ourselves on his sofa and he settled into an armchair facing us.

"Let me, Berta," Howard offered, taking my hand in his. "May I?" he asked the doctor. When the doctor nodded Howard went on to describe Jack's behavior and my violent reaction. "I think it scared both of us. We need your help, for Berta and me, and for what to do about Jack."

When he finished the doctor turned to me. "Is that how it felt to you, Roberta?"

"I just exploded out of control, like I used to. I haven't done that in a long time, you know that Dr. Fitz. What if I'd really hurt Jack? That's not me. How could I ever live with that? If I'd really hurt him?"

"No, that's not you, Roberta. I think we all know that." Dr. Fitzwater said. He sat quietly for a while. "Let's talk for a bit about Jack's behavior. What was it he did that triggered your reaction?"

"He started calling Howard names. Said he'd just married me so he'd have a nicer place to live and someone to wait on him." I looked at Howard and squeezed his hand. "And some other stuff I won't repeat. Doctor, Jack liked Howard and used to say he was a cool dude, and things like that. They were getting along fine, so I don't know what happened."

"Did anything happen between you and Jack, Howard?" The doctor peered at Howard.

"No, not a thing. This was just out of the blue. I can't understand it."

We all sat quietly for a few minutes. I could hear activity in the outer office, and the nurse stuck her head in to let the doctor know that the regularly scheduled patient had arrived.

"I'll just be a few minutes more," he replied. She nodded and quietly closed the door. "OK. Here's what we're going to do," he said. "First I'm writing you a prescription for a tranquilizer, Roberta. I want you to keep working on your anger management exercises and continue to keep our appointments." He went to his desk and wrote on a prescription pad. Tearing that off, he wrote another note.

"Also I'm giving you the name of a doctor who specializes in Borderline Personality Disorder. What you describe is called 'splitting', a classic behavior in many BPD patients. One day they think someone is wonderful and then overnight may take the opposite view. From that and the other things you've told me about Jack, I think that may be what he's suffering from. Of course that is not my specialty, so I can't be sure but I will call

Dr. Mayhew now and ask him to see Jack as soon as possible."

"But what if we can't get him to go? I've tried to get Jack to doctors before but he always refused."

"This is not negotiable, Roberta. He must get treatment or things will only get worse." The doctor was serious. He handed me the prescription papers.

"We'll get him there, Doctor." Howard stood up and pulled me to my feet. "Don't worry, honey, he'll go. I'll make sure of it."

As we were leaving, I could hear the Doctor on the phone, calling his colleague. We stopped on the way home to get the prescription filled and I took one of the pills as soon as I walked into the kitchen.

I can't ever remember having anyone to take care of a problem in my life. Steve had been gone much of the time, and I'd been single for many years. Everything had always been up to me and I always felt up to the task. So although I was happy for Howard's offer to take care of getting Jack to the doctor, I knew that it was my job and mine alone. I stiffened my spine and knocked softly on the door to Jack's room.

"We need to talk, Jack."

"Come in," Jack mumbled. He lay on his bed and looked warily at me as I opened the door.

"We can't go on like this, you know." I pulled a chair to the side of his bed and sat down.

"I know. You could'a killed me."

I skipped over that challenge. "I don't know if you know it, but I've been seeing a doctor. A psychiatrist. To help me with this anger that overtakes me sometimes."

"So?"

"I want you to see a doctor, too."

He started to sit up, the usual refusal almost visible at the tip of his tongue.

"No." I held up my hand in the 'stop' position. "You will go. This time you will go. I know you are as unhappy about your life as I am. This is a doctor who can help you take control of your life and make things better for you. You'd like that, wouldn't you?"

A noise behind me alerted me to Howard's arrival. I turned to look. He stood in the doorway and in answer to my unasked question he said, "Dr. Mayhew can see Jack this afternoon after office hours. I told him we'd be there."

Jack bolted upright on the bed. "No! I won't go. You can't make me." I could almost hear his eight year old voice refusing to brush his teeth or take a bath. The tranquilizer pill hadn't dialed me down, yet. My blood started to boil and I could feel my face turning red. Howard stepped forward and firmly took my arm just above the elbow, lifted me out of the chair and guided me toward the door.

"Jack and I will work this out, Berta. Why don't you go make a pot of coffee? We haven't even had breakfast yet."

Twenty minutes later all seemed quiet in Jack's room when Howard came into the kitchen and joined me at the table for coffee and a bowl of cereal. I started to protest his interference.

Howard held up his hand. "I know, my dear. You're thinking that all of this is your fault, and you should be able to handle it. But let me remind you of something. You and I are a team now. We have each other and can rely on each other. You have me and I have you. A team. That's the way a marriage works. Right?"

"Yeah, OK. But what happened? Is he going to go to the doctor?"

"Let's just say we had a man to man talk and Jack has agreed to see Dr. Mayhew this afternoon."

"How did you do that?" I was impressed. My past experiences with similar attempts had ended in loud but fruitless confrontations.

"You forget that I was a diplomat, my dear." His Cheshire cat expression of superiority was annoying, until he added, "Besides, the threat of bodily harm and homelessness can be very convincing." He chuckled then turned serious. "No, really, I just laid it out for him and we agreed it was for the best – for him as well as for you – and us."

At Howard's urging I packed a little picnic and we drove to the park a mile or so away. It was a beautiful spring day with warm breezes and fluffy white clouds flying high across a pale blue sky. It felt good to be out of the house, and in the fresh air. We found a picnic table away from the children's play area, overlooking a small lake where ducks and a swan glided peacefully. We strolled slowly around the lake, holding hands, then I unpacked our lunch and side by side on the bench we ate in companionable silence.

The tranquilizer had kicked in. I felt calm and relaxed. Shame, however, lay in wait at the back of my brain, muted but not deleted.

"Berta?"

"Yes, dear?"

"Tell me what you're thinking." Howard said. He was alternating potato chips with pickle chips, munching away while he gazed at a pair of squirrels chasing each other around the trunk of a nearby tree.

"Oh, it's all a muddle. I'm scared that I'm going crazy. I feel so bad that I've failed Jack. Most of all I can't see where it's all going to end, and I don't know what to do."

In the tree above where the squirrels were playing a robin perched, singing loudly. Telling the world something, I just didn't know what.

Howard put the cap back on the pickles and folded the potato chip bag closed. He swung one leg over to straddle the bench and faced me.

"Are you God?"

"What? Of course not. What do you mean?" The man did annoy me at times.

"Let me tell you who you are. May I?" Before I could reply he went on.

"You are an amazing woman, Roberta. You are good and kind. You are honest. You ran a successful organization serving young people. Even after retirement you still volunteer in the community and work to make yourself a better person." I started to protest. "Really, Howard, I...."

"No, I'm not finished." He reached over and took my hand. "You were given a stranger's child to rear, and you worked hard and did your best, but no matter what you did, nothing helped. You didn't know you were dealing with damaged goods, and thought everything that happened was your fault. You carry a load of guilt around with you that would flatten a world class weight lifter."

Everything he said was true. A single tear trickled down my cheek. Howard gently wiped it away with his thumb.

"Honey, it's time to face the truth. You're not God, and you can't fix Jack. I know you love him. I do, too, but he's a grown man now, not even a young man anymore. He needs professional help, and he must take on the responsibility for his own well-being, and for his own future."

"But what if….."

Howard interrupted. "I have a book that I want you to read. It saved my life when I lost Laura. It's called, *The Language of Letting Go* by Melody Beattie. "

"Let go and let God," I said. "Yes, that's in Al-Anon, too." I put my elbows on the table and my face in my hands. "I've never been very good at that."

"It's time, Berta. Now. I'll help you." Howard reached over with his left hand and used his strong fingers to massage my knotted neck. We sat that way for a long time. The squirrels were gone, and the robin too. The swan glided to the edge of the lake and waded up out of the water. A brief shake spun a rainbow of droplets, then the elegant bird settled on the grass and began to preen.

Chapter 17

Howard drove Jack to see Dr. Mayhew. I was eager to hear how things went and fussed about in the kitchen until they returned. Jack didn't even look at me when he came in, but went straight back to his room and closed the door. Howard's report was brief. Dr. Mayhew had seen Jack alone, and then asked to see Howard. His request, once he learned that Howard was not Jack's father, was for me to come see him. Soon. The first thing the next morning I called and made an appointment. The doctor would see me that very afternoon.

I approached his office with trepidation. What if it turned out that I was at fault for Jack's behavior? What if I'd done all the wrong things as his mother? I felt I was entering the wolf's lair, to be torn to pieces by a fierce and hungry animal.

Dr. Mayhew's office was a bit classier than Dr. Fitzwater's and the Doctor himself a bit more formal, and several years older, than Dr. Fitz. He wore a dark suit and tie, his hair was short – well, actually, he was nearly bald – but his round face exuded warmth and caring. He came from behind his desk to greet me, shaking and holding my hand for just a moment.

"Come in and sit down, there in the soft chair. I suspect you've been through hell, haven't you?" He sat nearby in a well-worn rocker, a clip board on his lap and a pen in hand. "Before I can help Jack – and he does need help – I need as much information as you can give me about him. Does that sound alright to you?"

"Yes, of course, Doctor. Anything you want to know." The information I'd given Dr. Fitzwater helped me repeat much of it to Dr. Mayhew. Jack's adoption, his childhood behavior of lying, cheating, stealing, his addictions to drugs and alcohol as he grew older. And his current behavior of 'splitting', of mood swings, and inability to manage money.

"Do you know, it never occurred to me that all this could be a...a 'condition'. A mental illness, I guess. I always thought I could make him change if I yelled louder and shook my finger harder. Now I feel so stupid. And so guilty." I slumped in my chair and shredded the tissue in my hands.

Dr. Mayhew said. "No, please. Don't feel bad. You had no way to know. And BPD is a complicated condition comprised of parts of so many other disorders like bi-polar, multiple addictions, and splitting, that it makes it difficult to diagnose. And, unfortunately, difficult to treat, although progress is being made in that area."

"But what causes it? Where does it come from? Is it hereditary?"

"We don't know. It could be genetic. Or if there has been abuse or neglect." Dr. Mayhew didn't ask the question, just looked at me with one slightly raised eyebrow.

"No, of course not. Well, I spanked him a few times but we loved him and I don't think Steve ever raised a hand to him. Ever." After a pause I added, "There were times I didn't like him very much, though."

We sat quietly, Dr. Mayhew and I. Both of us just thinking. I broke the silence. "There were a lot of separations. Might they have had the same effect on him?"

"Can you tell me about them?" His pen was poised over his clipboard.

"When he was four months old he was taken away from his foster family and given to us. Then just a few months later Steve left to go overseas and was gone for a year while Jack and I moved back to my home town to be near my parents. And I remember reading in Dr. Spock never to move a two year old child if it can be avoided, but of course we had no choice. Jack was two when Steve came home from Germany and we moved again, this time to Georgia."

Dr. Mayhew pondered this information; nodding, a thoughtful look on his face while he jotted some notes.

A memory flashed in my mind, a vignette so vivid I felt shocked.

"Oh, dear, I just thought of something. While Steve was gone I went up to Grand Rapids for three days to a regional meeting for my volunteer group. Jack stayed with our neighbors across the street. He played with their little girl all the time and they were happy to keep him for me. I thought he'd be glad to see me when I got home, but instead he pulled his little chair into a corner and sat there facing the wall. He wouldn't talk to me. Just sat there. It took several days before he got back to normal. I'd forgotten about that. Oh, dear."

I looked at Dr. Mayhew. "Could that be it? Was it my fault?"

"There's no way to know, Mrs. Thompson. But that's not the important thing now. The important thing now is to accept what is, and work to find a treatment that will help Jack live as close to a normal life as possible. It will be important to Jack that his mother is calm and carrying on her own activities as usual. You carrying a load of guilt, or trying to overcompensate by treating him differently, would not be helpful."

"I understand. Easier said than done though, I'll bet."

The doctor smiled. "I expect that's true, but you must try. The information you've given me about Jack is very helpful and I appreciate your coming in. Is it alright with you if I call Dr. Fitzwater and let him know about our conversation? He'll be able to work with you on any issues our talk today has raised for you. And I promise I'll do the very best for Jack that I can."

"That's fine. I can't tell you how much all this means to me. Thank you."

I left the doctor's office and drove to the park near home. I pulled into a parking place, turned off the motor and sat looking out at the little pond. I felt as if I were swimming up from the muddy bottom toward the light of the sun above. Did the pond seem prettier and the sun brighter than I'd seen them before? I knew things wouldn't change overnight, but there was hope. And hope is a good thing. Something I'd been without for a very long time.

Howard and I agreed that, for a time at least, I would back off and let Howard do the face to face stuff with Jack. He warned me, "I'm not playing Daddy, though, Berta. You guys need to be weaned from each other. You gotta stop punching each other's buttons. Capisch?"

"Yes, I understand, but it's going to be hard."

Weaning is not a simple process as any nursing mother can tell you. In the weeks to come Jack and I both went through some withdrawal pains. He started treatment with Dr. Mayhew and was able to get a new job with a lawn maintenance crew. Life at home smoothed out but wasn't perfect. I think we all longed for the time Jack could become independent enough to have his own place. 'One day at a time' I reminded myself regularly and often. My feelings of guilt were changing from regretting that I couldn't 'fix' Jack, to regretting that I'd been a fool not to listen to Julie and seek out the help earlier that may have made a big difference in his life.

Howard and I talked for hours and he helped me see that you can only do the best you can with the information you have and that guilt, like hate, only hurts the person feeling it.

"He's getting help, now, and he's getting better, can't you see that?"

"Yes, but…."

"Roberta, let go and let God, OK?"

I don't often talk to God but that night before I went to sleep I gave Jack to Him to care for. And then I thanked Him for the gift of Howard. The most precious gift I'd ever received.

Chapter 18

It was coming up on one year since little Lolo was born. Kenisha had returned to school in the fall while one of her neighbors cared for Lolo during the day. It was a difficult time but Kenisha worked hard at her studies and was doing well. In a few weeks summer vacation would begin and times would get easier for her, I hoped.

One Sunday afternoon Howard and I drove over to Roosevelt to visit and take Lolo's birthday present. It was interesting to watch Howard on these occasions. He'd park and start looking for someone nearby with whom to negotiate. A few words and a handshake and our car stayed as safe as if it were parked in our own driveway. How he was able to spot a responsible guard, I couldn't guess. Another handshake and the passing of a bill between palms occurred as we departed, although I didn't catch on to that part of the transaction right at first.

The physical appearance of Roosevelt Homes had not changed, but perceptions certainly had. We'd visited Kenisha often so our faces were familiar to the residents. I was no longer eyed with suspicion, and I no longer felt out of place or threatened. One of the things I loved about Howard was his way with people, all kinds of people. He must have been exceptional in his job, getting along and getting things done with people all around the world. As we made our way toward Kenisha's apartment through the crowd on the sidewalks he greeted many by name, and stopped to shake hands with several of the men and boys.

"Hey, Mz. Fischer. Hey, Mr. Fischer," a gaggle of women sitting on a staircase called as we passed by. Howard took my arm and pulled me to a halt.

"Now listen here, ladies, y'all know we're married now, right?" he asked them.

All the heads nodded in unison. "Yes sir," they chorused.

"So that means she has taken my last name now, right?"

"Yes sir," they chorused again.

He explained carefully that our name was Thompson. "Roberta Thompson and Howard Thompson. Now you got that?" He smiled at them, fairly oozing charm.

"Yesir." Teeth gleamed, heads bobbed.

"OK then. We're going to go visit Kenisha now. See y'all later."

As we turned away one voice rang out, clear as a trumpet. "Bye, Mz. Fischer." At Howard's look of disgust the chorus stomped their feet, slapped their knees and burst into cackles that would do a hen house proud.

Bless Howard. He laughed loudest of all.

Jerome opened the door to our soft knock and whispered that Lolo was sleeping and Kenisha would be out in just a minute.

What a difference from the first time I was here. Gone were the blankets blocking light from the windows. Gone the burnt brown shade on the lamp at the end of the shabby couch. Gone the couch itself. I'd replaced it with a nice one I found at a second hand furniture store along with a rug for the living room floor and a new lamp. Jerome, with Howard's help, had done a super job of repainting the rooms and fixing up a nursery in the corner of Kenisha's bedroom. The windows were clean and new curtains added cheerful color to all the rooms; Julie's and my effort to brighten the homecoming of the new mother and baby.

Kenisha's mother, home now from Rehab, came shuffling from the direction of the kitchen. She was thin as a stick and looked much older than her years. Her graying curls were shaved nearly to her scalp, her dark eyes darted about without looking directly at anyone.

"Howdy, folks. Howdy. You folks doin' OK today are you?" She seemed sober, but her hands were shaking. She clasped them together tightly while bobbing up and down in a half bow. "Come in, come in. Set yourselves down. On the couch there. We's enjoying that nice couch, Mz. Fischer. Sure are. Nish-a! Nish-a! You got company, honey." She settled herself in the one large armchair in the room. Kenisha emerged from the bathroom just as the baby started crying in the bedroom.

Jerome said, "I'll get her," and disappeared down the hall.

Suddenly the front door slammed open and Calvin charged in. He looked surprised when he saw us. "The'ell you doin' here?" he growled and, pushing past Kenisha, disappeared toward the kitchen.

This was not turning out to be the pleasant afternoon I had imagined. Howard rose to the occasion. "We thought we'd take Kenisha and Lolo out for a drive this afternoon, it's such a nice day. Maybe we can go to the park. Kenisha?"

Poor thing hadn't even had time to say hello, but she caught the cue, and promptly accepted. "That'd be nice. I'll get Lolo."

After I said hello to Mama I handed Lolo's gift to Howard and went to help Kenisha. In the bedroom Jerome was holding Lolo and apparently overheard the invitation.

"Thanks," he murmured in my ear. "I'll come meet you in the park – MLK – OK? I need to talk to you. Show 'em where, Nisha." With that he left to rejoin

Howard and Mama who were having a friendly sounding visit in the living room.

Jerome had graduated from high school and with the help of some scholarships was attending a local college. I knew his time at home was limited, along with his ability to keep an eye on things.

It took a little while to load up everything Lolo needed. Kenisha had her on one hip when she went to kiss her mother goodbye. "You take a nap now, Mama. You look tired. I love you."

"I love you, too, honey. Have a nice time now, y'all." Mama clung to Kenisha's hand before letting her go. She waved as we went out the door and I could see Calvin lurking in the shadows of the hall, watching us.

Martin Luther King Park is located close to the projects and appears to be designed for the exclusive use of its basketball playing residents. The courts were full of young and not so young men fully engaged in either making a basket or preventing someone else from doing the same. The talk and action were rough, and the laughter loud. Kenisha showed us to a small parking lot and we pulled in and waited there for Jerome.

Kenisha and I sat in the back seat and while we waited I played with Lolo and listened to Kenisha sing her praises. Lolo had grown into a pretty little girl and a curious one. Together we opened her gift, a story book with hopefully indestructible pages. We looked at the pictures until she lost interest and started to squirm in my lap.

"Mama," she said, lifting her arms toward Kenisha.

As I gave her up, Jerome arrived, opened the passenger door, and got in beside Howard. "Thanks," he said. "I wanted to see if I could find out what Calvin's up to, and make sure Mama was OK." After some discussion about where to go, Howard put the car in gear, rolled down Lincoln to the Interstate and out to our house in Kensington where Lolo could play and the rest of us could talk.

Kenisha disappeared to change a diaper and Jerome and Howard and I settled in the living room. The news Jerome reported was not good. Calvin was around a lot all of a sudden, and Mama was sober but very shaky and often confused. Kenisha was doing the best she could, but being the mother of a one year old when you're only fifteen yourself is beyond difficult.

"I really don't want to quit college," said Jerome. "But I don't get home 'til late and I don't like Kenisha being there alone with Mama and now Calvin. I don't know what to do." He sat with his elbows on his knees, his head in his hands.

Kenisha returned with a rejuvenated Lolo and put her down in the middle of the floor where she rolled into crawling position and began making 'house calls' on her adoring audience. She pulled herself up at our knees then plopped down, turned around and called on her next fan. She lightened the atmosphere in the room considerably.

Having overheard our conversation, Kenisha said, "Jerome worries too much. I'm only there after school and at night. I'm OK. And the neighbor ladies, they keep an eye on us, pretty much."

"Yes, but what about the summer? I'll still be in class most days and that leaves you there all day long. What about then?" Jerome's concern weighted his words.

"And what about Calvin?" I asked.

"I don't know 'bout Calvin. He don't...doesn't... hurt me or Lolo, but he's nasty and I don't like having him around."

Jerome added, "Something's going on with Calvin, I think. He might be in some kind of trouble. He talks meaner than usual and acts like someone might be following him, always looking over his shoulder and slinking around. And, yeah, he is nasty."

Howard suggested we order in a pizza, and Kenisha called her mama to tell her she and the baby would be home after supper. "We'll bring you some pizza," she promised. Jack appeared from his bedroom bringing Tigger and Boots with him. I didn't know he was at home. He settled on the floor with Lolo and with one little wooden block he and the cats kept her enthralled. He ignored the rest of us. The pizza arrived and while we ate the discussion continued but without ready answers leaping out at us.

All the ideas that surfaced resulted in "Yes, but….." answers. Many cost too much, others were logistically impractical.

Without preamble Jack spoke up from the floor. "For two people who call themselves 'movers and shakers', Mom, you guys suck."

Leaving behind the kittens and the little wooden block as well as an astonished and speechless audience, he got up and stalked off to his room.

There was a long silence.

"He's right, you know." Howard looked at me. "What we need is a vision with a capital V."

"Yes, he is, and yes we do." I replied. Drawing a long breath I announced, "It's time to get you home, Kenisha. I'm tired now so Howard can take you and Jerome back to Roosevelt while I rest and when he gets back here we'll put our heads together and make a plan. You'll see, it will be a great plan."

I had no idea what I was talking about, of course. I'd failed miserably with Jack and carried that guilt with me every day. I'd failed to change Kenisha's mind about keeping her baby and was eternally grateful for that failure. Lolo was the love of my life, well, besides Howard, of course. And now a new gauntlet had been thrown down; help Kenisha find a new and safe path to her and Lolo's future, and pretty quickly. We could not let the troublesome road blocks deter us, we must forge ahead.

Like a sudden wind, a burst of energy rushed through me. I clambered out of my recliner and went to the kitchen to start a pot of coffee. I placed a couple of pads of paper and some pens on the table plus Howard's brand new toy, a laptop computer. By the time he got home I'd established a command center that would make an army battalion commander proud, and was well into my second page of lists of things to do.

We divided our project into two parts. Short range and long range. Short range meant finding an immediate solution for Kenisha and Lolo. An improved housing situation, security from Calvin, help for her mother, and someone to assist Kenisha with the baby were all essential.

Long range meant solutions to all these same problems but ones that could be made permanent. After a lot of discussion Howard and I agreed that there should be a vision here that would include not only Kenisha, but Tasha and other girls as well. One that would include a safe place to stay with their children; that would make getting their education a priority, and that would provide an environment conducive to expanding their knowledge of and their participation in the larger community.

We had emptied the coffee pot, and the clock stood at 2 a. m. when we closed down our command post and headed for bed.

"I haven't had this much fun since I retired," declared Howard. I gave him a dirty look and punched him on the arm. "Except for that, of course," he blurted. He smiled and fell asleep before his head hit the pillow.

I fell asleep immediately, too. There was no barking, snarling black dog that night, nor would there ever be again.

Chapter 19

I met as soon as I could arrange it with Myra and Jean Jordon, her supervisor from Teen-Moms, and Valerie Messing, the case worker from Social Services to see if we could find some solutions to the problems surrounding Kenisha and her family. What soon became apparent was that although they were all sympathetic there was not much more that they could do. Burdened by thousands of cases, limited budgets, and exacting governmental guidelines, they were already doing as much as they could. I was disappointed, and said so. One good thing did come from Valerie, however. When I mentioned Calvin and our suspicions about his activities, she quickly volunteered to contact the police and see if she could find out more.

"We often work together with the police and I have a friend over there. I'll let you know what I learn," she said.

The quick fix for Kenisha's summer was to have her spend lots of time with us, but also to pay some of the neighbor ladies at Roosevelt to stay with Kenisha and her mama. They were happy to have a job, and Howard and I, with the help of 'Auntie' Gloria Swanson, carefully interviewed and selected reliable women. A daytime shift helped with housework and baby care. A night time helper slept over in case any help was needed then. I noticed that Valerie was checking up on the family more often than usual, too. Once when our paths crossed on the sidewalk at Roosevelt Homes I thanked her.

"I'm glad to do all I can," she replied. "And we thank you for all you're doing, too. By the way, I talked to my police friend about Calvin. He wouldn't tell me much, but I have the feeling there might be a big change in that boy's life, and soon."

Neither Howard nor I were wealthy, but we had both saved and invested our dollars carefully. Together we agreed that investing in Kenisha's and Lolo's futures was more important to us than all the 'Adventure Tours' and 'Senior Bus Trips' we might take. Plus we'd have more tangible returns on our investments than a scrapbook full of photographs.

And so the summer passed. Kenisha and Tasha had mended their friendship and spent lots of time together with their babies. We continued to employ the help Kenisha needed to keep her and the baby safe. Jack seemed to improve little by little and found he really liked his job with the landscaping company. He even started making some friends and occasionally brought a woman friend home to meet us.

Some memories are golden, etched in our minds forever. I remember that Labor Day as golden. It was a clear, beautiful day, still hot as summer wound down, but with just a touch of autumn coloring beginning to touch the trees and shrubs with dabs of yellow and orange. Howard and I had mentioned a backyard barbeque to the various folks we'd seen that week, but had no idea who, if anyone, would actually stop by. We prepared for an army, though, and it was good we did.

Kenisha and Lolo were there, of course, and Jack brought his friend, Shirley, a beautician he'd met in AA. Julie came with her new boyfriend, Tony, a veterinarian with his dog, Justice. Jerome drove up, bringing Tasha and Mikey, and all the neighbors dropped over, too. Howard commanded the grill and served up hamburgers and hotdogs on request. We drank lemonade and I brought out a big casserole dish of baked beans, and a huge bowl of salad greens to put on the picnic table with the other 'fixins'. Everyone served themselves.

The no-longer kitties, Boots and Tigger, were there and chased Justice, who chased them back. All three stopped often to visit Howard and sniff hopefully at the grilling meat. Mikey and Lolo chased the cats and the dog, and the mommies chased the toddlers. Occasionally Lolo would climb up in her 'Nana's' lap for a hug and a bit of rest. I loved being 'Nana'. Even Kenisha called me

Nana now. The grownups mixed and mingled, praising the beauty and intelligence of the children, and swapping stories of their own childhood adventures. Great hoots of laughter broke out from time to time.

I lay back in a chaise lounge and watched the show. It was a picture I'd hold in my mind for the rest of my life - a kaleidoscope of skin color and religion and culture. But still, a family. My family.

Kenisha dropped Lolo in my lap and plopped onto the grass beside me. She was growing into a lovely young lady, Kenisha was. She was a good mommy, but also a serious student with goals for her future. The goals changed often; from becoming a clone of one of her favorite people like Tamika or the library lady or the vet tech, to being a model or a movie star, to more scholarly pursuits; doctor, lawyer, maybe even merchant chief. The world was opening up for her and whatever the future held, I knew it did not include places like Roosevelt Homes.

She looked at the friends crowding our yard, then looked at me and grinned. "I was wrong, wasn't I? When I said that having a baby is the only way to have something to love that will love you back."

"And I was wrong when I thought you should give up your baby. I can't imagine loving anyone more than I love Lolo." The very thought brought a tear to my eye. "And you," I added, leaning over and hugging her.

Just then Howard dragged over a chair and sat down with us. "Can I get some of that?"

"With the possible exception of this man," I added, reaching to take his hand.

We continued working on a long-range plan for Kenisha and other young mommies like her. We gathered all the information we could about available services for under privileged pregnant youngsters and spent many hours interviewing school officials and social workers to ensure we were not re-inventing a wheel, and also to enlist their help in our plan. We even talked to the Mayor and City Council members to keep them apprised of our ideas and progress.

As Howard and I drove around town making our calls we kept noticing a vacant old two story house not far from the projects with a For Sale sign in the yard. A relic that had seen better days, it reminded me of myself a bit: old, but with quite a few good miles left on it yet. An iron fence guarded the overgrown front yard but the gate hung loose on one hinge. A wide wrap-around porch called out for children to play there. The house itself was built of red brick. Once-white shutters sagged beside large, boarded-over windows that promised large rooms inside. One day in late October we stopped to give it a closer look.

I tested each step to the porch carefully before putting my full weight on it. They held firm. Once there I turned to look out at the neighborhood. Other homes on the block had small signs in their front yards or in a window. One said 'Dr. Roberts, Dentistry', another said just 'Income Tax', and yet another said 'Baptist Ministries'. If we could make this into our learning center we'd be in good company.

I turned around to look at the house. "What do you think?" I asked Howard.

"Come here." He had found a loose board where we could peek inside. I shuffled through mounds of dry leaves and he moved over so I could look in. It was dark, but I could see a large room with a high ceiling and with stairs on one wall going to the second story. A double-door on the opposite wall opened into the entry way, and a door in the back wall stood ajar, but I couldn't see beyond it. Peeling wall paper hung from the walls, and the floor was littered with the debris from other life-times; papers, a book, an abandoned valise, a bent and dented saucepan.

"Let's walk around the building, and see what else we can see. I got the name and number of the realtors from the sign so we can call for a full tour if we want to."

Howard took my hand and we walked on the porch around the side of the house and down some smaller steps to the over-grown yard. The back yard was large and bright with a couple of tall oaks dressed in bronze and some smaller sugar maples dripping bright red leaves. A thick hedge enclosed the space. A perfect playground. The back of the house bulged out with a sunroom, and kitchen windows opened high above our eye level. I knew that old homes could be nightmares waiting to happen, but on the surface the house looked sturdy.

I looked at Howard. He grinned back.

"I think this may be the place," he said. "I'll call the realtor." When we got home he did, and made an appointment for a day in mid-November. We were both excited.

Chapter 20

On a Saturday afternoon in early November Howard and I decided to stop by Roosevelt Homes and talk with Kenisha and her mother about our Thanksgiving plans. We were envisioning a houseful of friends and family gathered around a bountiful table to celebrate our many blessings. We planned to ask them to join us.

We parked in our usual spot and Howard looked around to find a suitable car watcher. It was a clear, bright day, not too cold, but the sidewalks and steps were unaccountably empty of the usual residents so we left the car locked but unattended. There was an empty police car parked across the street. We paid no attention to the sirens wailing in the distance. They are common in this part of town.

Howard said, "Well, they know it's us, so I think it will be OK. I wonder where everyone is, though."

"Like they're having a party and didn't invite us."

"Yeah, right." He smiled at me, and squeezed my hand. We made our way along the sidewalk and across in front of one of the buildings.

"You don't wanna go up there right now," a voice from one of the doorways warned. We stopped and tried to find where the voice was coming from. "There's trouble up there. Don't go." I saw one door cracked open about an inch with a dark face behind it.

"What's wrong?" Howard asked.

"The po-lice is there. Trouble. Go home."

We looked at each other. "We have to get Kenisha and Lolo," I murmured to Howard. I could see his jaw tighten and he nodded.

"I'll go," he said. "You stay here."

"No, if you go, I go. They need our help and I don't trust that Calvin."

He capitulated, but his unease was visible. "We'll be careful," he told the voice behind the door but it was already closed. We could hear the snick of the lock being turned.

We hurried up the steps and walked along the balcony to Kenisha's apartment. I wished I had my collapsible cane with me. The door to Kenisha's apartment stood ajar just a little.

"You stay back," Howard whispered in my ear, pushing me back toward the corner of the building. Then he stepped forward and knocked. "Hey! Anyone home?"

"Yeah. Come on in," a male voice answered. Howard pushed on the door and edged cautiously across the threshold. I was right behind him

Suddenly the door swung wide and banged against the inside wall. One of Calvin's buddies, Bobby, I think, grabbed Howard and pulled him in, then took my elbow with one hand and motioned us inside with a gun in his other hand.

"Yeah, we's home. Come on in. Join the party." The weapon accentuated the invitation. He slammed the door shut and locked it behind us.

The scene in that small apartment is impressed indelibly on my brain. Blankets again hung at the windows blocking out daylight and preventing anyone from seeing in. The feeble light in the room came from an overhead fixture in the ceiling. The furniture was pushed back against the walls except for the couch which was turned to face the door. It held Kenisha and Lolo and Mama. I stumbled over a police officer who lay just inside the door, motionless, in a pool of blood. A second officer huddled in the middle of the room, his hands tied behind his back and with masking tape plastered across his mouth. His eyes bugged out, his blinks trying to send a desperate message. Calvin stood over him with a gun pointed at his head.

"Yo, come on in, honkies." Calvin exuded bravado, but his face was gray and the hand holding the gun shook. "Go sit on the couch by Kenisha. And keep your mouths shut unless you want them taped shut like him." He waved the gun and the officer cringed.

Quickly Howard knelt by the downed officer and put his fingers on the base of his neck, feeling for a pulse. He looked up at me, and gave a tiny shake of his head.

"I said get over there on the couch, honkey-man. Now!"

On the couch Kenisha was rocking back and forth, back and forth, holding a screaming Lolo. Kenisha, too, was a pale shade of gray. "Do what he says, Mr. Howard. Please." Mama was frozen in place beside Kenisha.

"OK, OK, Calvin, I'm going. Stay cool." Before taking a perch on the arm of the couch, Howard patted first Mama then Kenisha, "It's OK, we're going to be OK."

I squeezed in between Kenisha and her mama who was bobbing her head, rolling her eyes and moaning over and over, "Jesus, oh precious Jesus. Jesus, oh precious Jesus."

"Hey, Calvin," Howard said, as if we'd just come to visit. "Looks like you've got yourself a situation here."

"You could say that," Calvin sneered. "What you gonna do about it, huh?"

"Let us take Kenisha and the baby and your mama out of here. They don't need to be seeing all this." He gestured at the obscene sight of the dead officer lying in a pool of blood and his bound and gagged partner who lay at our feet.

"You crazy sumbitch. They're my ticket out of this shithole, you think I'm going to let you take them? Think again." He paced in a circle around the room.

"Well, how about you let them and Roberta go, and keep me as your hostage. That's all you need, isn't it? A hostage?"

I gasped at the idea, and frowned at Howard.

Bobby stuck in his two cents. "Yeah, Calvin, then we wouldn't have to listen to all that screamin'."

"Shut up!" Calvin shouted at us on the couch. "Just shut up! You, too," he added to Bobby. "I know what I'm doin'."

I put one arm around Mama. With my other hand I patted Kenisha on her leg. "Just keep calm," I urged quietly. "We'll be OK."

Howard picked up the refrain. "Let's all keep calm so nobody else gets hurt."

My ears picked up some noise from outside, like heavy boots trying to tiptoe stealthily. Leather squeaked, and metal clinked. Inside everyone froze and listened. Calvin jumped to the space behind the couch where he faced the door, his hostages creating a living shield in front of him.

"Don't nobody be a hero, now, ya' hear?" he warned. He directed Bobby to join him behind the couch.

"Calvin? We know you're in there. Come out peacefully and we can end this here and now," a voice blared through a bullhorn.

With no hesitation at all, Calvin raised the gun and fired at the door. The shot assaulted our ears it was so close, and the bullet blasted a hole exactly where the voice had come from. Mama screamed and Lolo screamed louder. Kenisha bit her lips and groaned. Howard and I looked at each other. I gritted my teeth to keep from screaming, too. I'd never been so frightened in my life. Even Howard flinched at the gunshot, but his face looked grim and determined. He put his arm around Kenisha.

"There are women and children in here," he called out.

"That's right, fools. I got me five, no six hostages in here. And I got some demands. Some de-mands, you hear me?" Calvin threw out his challenge like a gauntlet, engaging battle with the enemy. To Howard he said, "And you, you shut up. I'm in charge here."

We could hear feet shuffling around outside on the walkway. A new voice spoke up from just outside the door. It was Jerome.

"Calvin, it's me. What are you doin', man?" The door knob rattled. "Let me in. We need to talk about this."

"No, no more talk. Tell the assholes I want a car and, uh, $100, no $200,000 and safe passage outa here for me and Bobby. When you got that, then we'll talk. Hear me?"

"I'm serious, bro. Don't get yourself in any deeper. We can work things out. And let the women and Lolo loose. They don't deserve any of this. Please, Calvin. Hand them out to me and I'll see that they are safe." Jerome was pleading.

I thought Calvin was about to let Mama, Kenisha and the baby go out to Jerome when the disembodied voice blared again. "Give it up, Calvin. There's no good way out of this."

Blam! Another shot hit the door. A cry from Jerome, "Jesus, Calvin, you hit me!" We could hear voices and footsteps moving away along the balcony. That's when I became terrified. Not frightened, not scared to death......terrified. Glancing behind me, I could see that Calvin was losing control of himself and the situation.

"A car and $200,000" he screamed. "No more talk." Sweat stained his shirt and poured off his face. "Bobby, take Nisha and Mama and the baby back to Nisha's room." As they stumbled off toward the bedroom he brandished his gun at me and Howard and added, "Honkies, you stay there." Howard slid off the arm of the couch and moved over beside me, taking my hand.

We were planted between the gun-happy devil behind us and heavily armed law enforcement on the other side of the door in front of us.

It was quiet outside. I could hear Kenisha in the bedroom murmuring to a whimpering Lolo while the rocking chair creaked rhythmically.

We settled in to wait. I knew it might take hours because I'd seen it on all those cop shows on TV. The phone rang and Calvin talked, but held fast to his demands. He allowed Kenisha access to the kitchen in order to feed Lolo, but ordered Bobby to keep a close eye on her. The rest of us got nothing to eat or drink. Except for the bound and gagged officer who remained crumpled on the floor, we were allowed to visit the windowless bathroom one by one, again with Bobby standing guard in the hallway. The small apartment stank with the smell of fear, perspiration, urine, dirty diapers and gun smoke. Howard and I huddled together on the couch. I drew strength and courage from the bulk and warmth of his body.

The phone talks continued, and after nearly three hours Calvin said to Bobby, "Stand back here and keep your gun on fancy folk here. I gotta pee." They exchanged places, and Calvin went into the bathroom and closed the door. Bobby stood behind us, brandishing his weapon from his new position of power.

I was getting really hungry and thirsty. Hoping that Bobby might be too, I kept my voice low and suggested that perhaps some take-out food and bottled water would be available if we asked for it.

"Shut up, old lady!" he snarled. But when Calvin returned from the bathroom Bobby said, "Hey, Calvin, how about we get some food and water up here? I'm hungry, and sure could use a drink."

To my surprise Calvin picked up the phone and called the negotiator. "I want some food and water sent up here, now!" he demanded. "And where's my ride and my money? I'm getting tired of waiting." To emphasize his request he fired the gun into the ceiling. "Next time, I'm shooting one of these honkies, so speed it up!"

They must have anticipated Calvin's request for food and water as very soon the phone rang again to announce its arrival. "Go stand by the door, bro," Calvin said. "and when they knock open it just enough to get the stuff inside."

"Calvin, how about having them remove the dead officer while they're up here? He's beginning to stink real bad and he's right there by the door." Howard voice was low and calm. As he spoke he turned to look at Calvin and when he turned his head back again his lips brushed my ear. "If anything happens get down on the floor, fast," he whispered. He cut his eyes at the officer alive at our feet and I noticed for the first time that the young man had managed to maneuver into a sitting position and was sideways to us, and very close. His eyes darted at his shirt pocket, where the key to the handcuffs resided, I assumed. I shifted forward to shield him from Calvin's view and to see if I could reach that pocket. Howard leaned forward, too.

Calvin was on the phone again, pacing back and forth, and while his attention was focused elsewhere I slipped my hand into the pocket and retrieved the key. I palmed it to Howard who watched Calvin move around the room to direct the removal of the body and the delivery of food and water by two officers in bullet-proof vests, helped by Bobby. Quickly Howard unlocked the cuffs and the officer flexed his hands, but continued to hold them behind his back so Calvin wouldn't notice.

What came next remains a blur in my mind. Just as the door closed behind the officers something rolled into the room and exploded. There was a blinding flash, a loud explosion, and a bloom of choking smoke engulfed us. Instantly the door caved in and armed men in helmets and gas masks invaded the room. I rolled onto the floor and tried unsuccessfully to get under the couch. Howard crouched over me; a human shield. The officer we had freed was gone, I couldn't see where. That's when shots were fired, and I could hear shouted curses and sounds of scuffling. Howard jerked, then lay still, pinning me to the floor.

Our young officer had charged Bobby and disarmed him, but Calvin in a last desperate act pulled the trigger even as he was killed himself.

I could hear screaming from the bedroom; Kenisha, Lolo and Mama were all venting their terror. Someone close by was screaming too, and I only realized it was me when Howard's body was lifted from mine and strong, gentle hands picked me up and helped me walk down the hallway to Kenisha's bedroom. I hugged Kenisha and we cried together. I don't think she knew that Howard was dead. Howard, dead. I couldn't tell her because I wouldn't let myself believe it, yet.

Myra and Valerie from Social Services soon arrived and efficiently packed what belongings were needed to leave that horrendous place. Conversations were held, promises made, and all I could hear was noise. Garbled noise that made no sense to me.

Hostage situations are not supposed to end that way.

Chapter 21

I remember nothing else until I was at home standing in the shower, washing away the blood and smells of that awful day. Julie was at the house, as was Jack, but I saw them through a dark veil of horror and grief. They made me eat some soup but it tasted awful in a mouth still filled with gunsmoke and the odors of death. I found my tranquilizers, took two, and lay on the bed. Without Howard beside me I never expected to sleep peacefully again. When I woke up Tigger was snuggled up beside me and Boots warmed my back. Julie was sitting in a chair beside the bed. I took her hand and we cried silently together. Jack came in and sat on the edge of the bed. "I'm sorry, Mom. God, I am so sorry." He cried, too. It registered that this was the second time I heard those words from Jack.

Just as it had after my house fire, it took a while to sort things out. First there was Howard's funeral. I was surprised to see the mayor and some city council members and others we had approached about our project for pregnant teens. An old bus brought a large group of somber residents from Roosevelt Homes, including the gentleman who had tried to warn us away that awful day. Our neighbors were all there, shock still registering on their faces. Howard's two sons flew in as well as some dignitaries from the USAID organization in D. C. Apparently Howard was higher up the ladder there than he'd ever let on to me. Myra and others from Teen Moms and Social Services filled one row of chairs. Julie and Jack and Kenisha and Jerome, with a bandaged arm, sat with me. It was the saddest day of my life, but at the same time I was proud that this diverse group of people came together to honor Howard's life. He'd touched many lives. Not the least of which was my own.

***

It took an endless round of conversations with the police to help put together what had happened in that dark apartment in Roosevelt Homes that day. There were depositions and inquests. Whose decision it was to throw in the smoke bomb was questioned extensively and blame eventually placed on the leader of the Swat Team. The negotiator had warned against it. It didn't matter to me. Nothing was going to bring Howard back.

The young officer came to call to apologize for not saving Howard's life. His name was Frank Hollingsworth and I could tell his anguish was almost as acute as mine. But we had shared that life changing experience and neither of us would ever forget it. I promised him he had done the very best he could, and what happened was not his fault.

Kenisha's mama hit the bottle hard, suffered a relapse and returned to Rehab shortly after Calvin's quick and very quiet funeral. Jerome won a good athletic scholarship and headed off for the University of Tennessee where he lived in the athletes' dorm. Kenisha and Lolo stayed with Auntie Gloria during the time I was going through my worst days. Finally, though, they moved to my house where Jack and I re-arranged ourselves to accommodate a young mother and a lively little girl.

Kenisha and Tasha stayed in school and their children thrived in a day care center nearby. It was my pleasure to foot the bill for that.

AFTERWORD

When Howard died I thought I would die, too. But I remember him saying "What we need is a Vision with a capital V." We had worked hard to develop that vision and the idea for the Learning Center and Nursery School had taken shape. I had to put it all on hold, however, as I struggled to recover.

By the time the Center opened, Lolo was four, and Kenisha was a freshman at the local college. She worked part-time at the big library downtown. Tamika became the first Development Director of the Center, raising the money that was needed to keep the operation going. She was a popular speaker in all the civic clubs and women's organizations around town and was able to approach any of the area's 'movers and shakers' with confidence and style.

Lolo and Kenisha stilled lived with me, although I did hire a fulltime nanny/housekeeper to keep things going. Jack finally moved out and seemed to be doing well on his own. His new job as an animal handler at a veterinary clinic seemed perfect for him and he tended a small vegetable garden and grew roses at his apartment.

On the third anniversary of his death we dedicated 'The Howard Thompson Learning Center and Nursery School'. The renovated building stood proudly among its neighbors. The fence, the porch, the shutters were all repaired and repainted, and the grounds had been groomed to a 'T'. The first floor with its large, bright rooms belonged to the nursery school and was filled with toys and playpens and cribs....and toddlers. The second floor was for the young mothers and their newborns and also housed meeting rooms and the offices of Teen Moms. The Center was staffed 24 hours a day for the girls who came for a few days or longer when their home life, like Kenisha's, became chaotic.

At the dedication ceremony, attended by friends and dignitaries and clients mixed in an eclectic crowd gathered in front of the building, I read an excerpt from a poem called ***"Some People"*** by Flavia Weedn that is framed and hanging in the entrance hall:

Gail Kiracofe

Some people come into our lives

and leave footprints on our hearts

and we are never ever the same.

Some people come into our lives

and quickly go... Some stay for a while

and embrace our silent dreams.

Some people come into our lives

and they move our souls to sing

and make our spirits dance.

They help us to see that everything on earth

is part of the incredibility of life...

and that it is always there

for us to take of its joy.

Some people come into our lives

and leave footprints on our hearts

and we are never ever the same.

"That was Howard," I said. "Howard and all of you who have helped to make this happen. Thank you. I can feel Howard's presence here right now, and I know he is as proud and happy on this occasion as I am."

I put an arm around Kenisha and hugged her, and watched as our family gathered around us. Jack, Jerome, Tasha and Mikey, Myra and Julie. And of course, Lolo. We had lots of 'someones' to love who loved us right back.

THE END

About the Author

Gail Kiracofe lives in a retirement community in Virginia where she keeps in touch with the real world via computer, tablet, e-reader, and video/movie streaming. Not your average old lady, she led a full and fascinating life from which she draws material to write essays, memoir pieces, and a bit of political commentary. ***Someone to Love*** is her first novel.

22997323R00123

Made in the USA
Charleston, SC
07 October 2013

Gift

JAN 2 8 2014